THE PROMISE

"Give me back my gun, mister," the Kid said. "You got no right taking what's mine."

Smiling, Zach handed the Smith & Wesson back to the young man. "You keep it in that holster now, hear?"

"You'll get yours, mister," the Kid snarled. "You got it coming. That's a promise."

THE RETURN OF ZACH STUART
A Berkley Western Original by
WILL KNOTT

Berkley Books by Will C. Knott

RED SKIES OVER WYOMING
RETURN OF ZACH STUART

WILL C. KNOTT

THE RETURN OF ZACH STUART

BERKLEY BOOKS, NEW YORK

THE RETURN OF ZACH STUART

A Berkley Book / published by arrangement with the author

PRINTING HISTORY
Berkley edition / July 1980

For information address: Berkley Publishing Corporation, 200 Madison Avenue, New York, New York 10016.

ISBN: 0-425-04600-1

A BERKLEY BOOK® TM 757,375

PRINTED IN THE UNITED STATES OF AMERICA

Prologue

A RIDER GALLOPED OUT of the moonless night and clattered down the hard-packed Main Street of Canyon City. Crossing the railroad tracks at the south end of town, he swept along the tracks toward a large house set back in among a grove of cottonwoods. Into the trees he plunged, pulling up in front of Miss Helen's Parlor House so abruptly that he almost lost the frail burden slung across the pommel of his saddle.

In the dim glow that came from the single red lamp sitting in Miss Helen's window, the man's features loomed satanically. His brow was high and square, clearly visible in the reddish light. His mouth was an unforgiving line framed by a black, drooping mustache, his jaw square and resolute. Dark, gleaming eyes peered out from under craggy brows. It was the face of a man consumed by an ungovernable wrath.

Pulling from his holster a huge Dragoon, he pumped two thunderous shots into the night. The door of Miss Helen's was flung open. The mistress of the place stood in the doorway, the folds of her pink robe held in place by one hand, a lantern clutched in the other.

"Miss Helen!" the rider shouted with hoarse fury, "I have brought you a cyprian worthy of your infamous house!"

It was a young woman the rider had flung over his

pommel. Plunging his revolver back into his holster, he grabbed the woman's abundant shock of rich auburn hair and threw her bodily from the horse. The woman landed heavily, rolled over once, and came to rest on her back, her arms flung wide. The rider drove his rowels cruelly into his mount's flanks, wheeled his horse about, and galloped off through the cottonwoods.

Miss Helen was already running down the porch steps to the crumpled figure. Placing the lantern on the ground beside the body, she peered into the bruised, swollen face. The girl groaned and opened her eyes. The sight of Helen's face looming so close in the darkness caused her to flinch away. She uttered a tiny, frightened cry.

"It's all right," Helen told the girl softly, reassuringly. "He's gone."

"He thinks I'm dead!" the girl cried piteously. "Don't let him know the truth! Hide me! Please!"

Helen turned her head. Jane Durrell and Sophie were standing in the open doorway. "Help me get her inside!" Helen cried. "Hurry!"

The two girls hurried down the steps. The three of them carried the girl inside and placed her down on a small day bed in a room off the parlor. The rest of the girls were crowding down the staircase by this time. Miss Helen left the room and told them to get back upstairs. It was close to dawn and they would need their sleep. The weekend was coming. As the girls turned and stumbled excitedly back up to their rooms, Helen went back to the injured girl.

Jane's face was grim. She turned to Helen. "Look at her back!" she whispered angrily.

They had taken off the girl's torn, blood-streaked bodice, revealing shoulders lacerated with broad, red stripes that reached down across her narrow back, clear to her buttocks. The welts were inches wide and so deep they resembled aggravated brands. Frowning angrily, Helen pulled off the girl's torn skirt and petticoat, the bloodstained chemise. The girl had not worn a corset and as soon as her slim body was naked, Helen knew why.

"My God!" gasped Jane. Behind them, Sophie began to weep.

The girl was pregnant; pretty far along, in fact, her slim figure the kind that did not advertise pregnancy until well into the seventh or eighth month.

"Get the doctor, Sophie," Helen said, without looking back. "And hurry!"

As Sophie darted from the room, Helen smoothed the girl's rich auburn curls off her forehead and looked down into her youthful face. Both cheekbones were darkened from bruises and one of her luminous brown eyes was swollen shut. Bruises about her neck convinced Helen that the girl had been throttled by powerful hands. Her thighs, too, were darkening visibly as the bruises began to set. She looked as if she had been dragged a considerable distance.

Shaking her head in disbelief, Helen reached back for the blanket folded at the foot of the bed and swiftly, gently covered the pitifully battered body.

"Do you know her?" Jane asked Helen, her voice hushed.

Helen nodded. "She's Dudley Stuart's wife."

"The owner of the Slash D?"

"That's the one. The owner of the Slash D. The biggest, most powerful rancher in this valley." Helen turned to look at Jane. "You know him. You've seen him here. He's that tall, lean man with the broad shoulders and powerful voice, the one that always asks for Sadie."

"Oh, yes. I know him." Jane looked in wonder back at the girl, who was beginning to moan softly. "Shouldn't we send a rider out to his place to fetch him?"

"No need," said Helen, looking back down at the girl.

"But why not?"

Miss Helen waited a moment before replying, then took a deep breath, as if it were difficult for her to form the words. "Because he's the son of a bitch who done this to her, that's why. He's the one who threw her off his horse and left her here!"

Abruptly her composure vanished. Helen bowed her face in her hands and began to weep softly.

One

ZACH STUART STARED OUT through the rain-streaked window, at the grassland sliding past. He had seen this cattle country only once before, when he had been brought here by his mother. Only that time it had not been raining.

It had been a secretive journey and Zach remembered vividly the precautions his mother had taken to see to it that no one in Canyon City got more than a glimpse of her as Jane Durrell bundled her into the carriage and drove them through town and across the tracks to Jane's place.

At that time, Zach recalled, he had been impressed by the sight of the snowcapped peaks that rimmed the valley, seeming to hang above the town like some fabulous tapestry. Zach had noticed also the bustle of the place, the smell of new lumber and the look of recently shingled roofs and brightly painted clapboards, all of which testified to the cattle town's booming prosperity.

Zach caught a glimpse of the Little Whiskey River just ahead. Its long, lazy loops gleamed dully under the leaden sky, the steady rainfall mottling its broad surface. The train's wheels clicked over the bridge spanning the river, and despite the rain Zach glimpsed the tiled roof of the train station. Idly, Zach turned his head and peered through the rain, trying for a glimpse of the mountain range he knew hung over the valley. But it was hidden by the impenetrable curtain of rain that pelted almost straight down out of low, glowering clouds. It was a good, soaking, needed spring rain, just one more reason why the grasslands in this valley were so lush.

The conductor entered the coach and announced their arrival in Canyon City. Zach rose from his seat. Snugging down his Stetson, he started for the door. He was a tall, lanky, broad-shouldered man with a shock of dark hair that bunched out from under the sweatband of his hat and coiled luxuriantly down onto his neck. His face was lean and surprisingly resolute for a man still in his twenties. His jaw was square, the brows and cheekbones prominent, his dark eyes burning with a quiet but forbidding intensity. His face was burnished by wind and sun to a rough, leathery consistency, and spoke eloquently of his years in the saddle.

He was dressed for train travel now in a black, worsted frock coat and vest, his pants tucked into the tops of his worn but well-cared-for cordovan leather riding boots. A white broadcloth shirt gleamed from beneath his vest; a black string tie was knotted at his neck.

He had to duck his head to get through the coach's doorway, and he stood silently beside the conductor as he waited for the train to come to a stop. Zach glimpsed upturned faces on the platform—expectant, eager—most of them peering out from under gleaming umbrellas. But Zach was looking for no one, expected no one. The train creaked, then squealed to a stop. The conductor hopped down with his stool. Zach descended lightly, emerging into the warm, steady rain without flinching. He shouldered his way carefully through the light throng crowding close upon the halted coaches.

A four-wheeled flatbed cart had already been brought up to the baggage car. Zach asked one of the attendants for his gear—a Winchester and a large, grained leather gladstone. Then he stood back to watch as the ebony coffin was unloaded onto the baggage cart.

A small, mournful-looking man sidled soundlessly up

beside Zach and cleared his throat. "Mr. Stuart?"

Zach turned. The undertaker was wearing a black derby and a black, severely tailored suit. He did not carry an umbrella. The rain was dripping from the rim of his derby. The little man was holding out a sodden business card.

Zach took the card from him and glanced at it. "You're Skelkins?"

"Yes."

The undertaker turned his attention to the ebony coffin. Unprotected now, its silver fittings gleamed in the rain. One of the station attendants was throwing a blanket over it.

"My people will be here soon," Skelkins said. "Allow me to handle all the details. Miss Durrell has given me what information I need. The burial is set for Wednesday, at nine in the morning."

Zach looked back at the coffin. Three days, he realized, should be plenty of time. Looking back at Skelkins, Zach nodded curtly, lifted the gladstone and his rifle, and walked across the platform through the rain. He found a large station wagon leaving for The Canyon City Hotel, and climbed in.

It was still raining two hours later when Zach shouldered his way through the batwings of the Belle Fourche Saloon. The rain's insistent drumming on rooftops and boardwalks, the sight of the street transformed into fetlock-deep guagmires was oppressive to him now. The damp, crowded interior of the saloon stank with the smell of wet, unwashed bodies, and the faint but unmistakable stench of horse manure that had been tracked into the saloon and was now mixed with the no-longer-fresh sawdust that covered the floor. Heavy coils of cigar smoke hung in the air.

Few paid attention to Zach as he spotted a table along one wall and headed for it. Two of the saloon's girls were circulating listlessly between the tables, taking orders and smiling without enthusiasm at the broadly suggestive remarks that came their way. When a girl eventually found her way to his table, Zach ordered a beer. Then he chucked his tan Stetson back off his forehead and looked around.

The Belle Fourche was the biggest saloon in town and obviously the most popular. It was only three in the afternoon, and already the place was crowded. The bar was of solid mahogany, one of the longest Zach had ever seen. A mirror behind it extended the bar's full length, reflecting not only the glasses and bottles that sat on the shelves, but also the two large chandeliers that lit the place. Above the mirror was a large mural, entitled *The Cowboy's Dream*. Gamboling in a secluded forest pool were four nude, well-endowed, and somewhat oversized nymphs. As they splashed about in the water, they glanced coyly back over their ivory shoulders at the bar's patrons. Their shapely posteriors were boldly presented, and two of the nymphs found it impossible to shield from view entirely their ample breasts. The artist's colors throughout were lavish and spectacular, even when viewed through the saloon's dense, smoky atmosphere.

The green felt tops of poker tables glowed softly in the dimmer recesses of the saloon. Still further back a small crowd of players were hovering over the roulette wheel, while another group was bent over the craps table alongside.

The girl brought Zach his stein of beer. With genuine pleasure Zach took it from her and drank deeply. He felt his shoulder muscles relaxing as his tension eased. Leaning back, he put the stein down and began watching the men before him standing up to the bar. At first the murmur of voices was broken only by an occasional boisterous remark; quiet laughter with some backslapping predominated. It was a comforting, relaxing sound. Gradually, however, Zach became aware that one of the bar's patrons was making no effort to keep his voice down and was speaking to the smaller man beside him in what was a deliberately abusive manner. The taller one was obviously spoiling for a fight.

When Zach saw the rest of the bar's patrons edge away, he realized that only three men were involved in the argument. The fellow who was the target of the surly comments was smaller than the other two. He was a red-faced fellow with sandy hair and a doggedly belligerent cast to his face. His voice was not as powerful as his taller antagonist's, but it was almost as loud and was more like a perpetual whine than anything else.

The taller fellow was in his late forties, a graying man with mean little eyes, a hawklike nose and a powerful square jaw. Though his girth was more than ample, it looked as solid and as formidable as an oak tree.

Alongside this man was his sidekick—a smaller, younger man with a surprisingly pallid face, cold gray eyes, and long, stringy dark hair that ran down onto his shoulders. He wore his black, flat-crowned hat well back on his head. His body was as slender and lithesome as a girl's, making his heavy gunbelt with its oversized Colt hanging from it appear obscenely inapropriate. There was no doubt in Zach's mind that this beardless kid not only knew how to use his weapon, but gained considerable pleasure from doing so.

The sandy-haired fellow's unpleasant voice cut through the now tense silence: "No! Slash D *can't* use that pasture, Nate—and you can tell that son of a bitch he's pushed to his limit! That Sweetwater Range belongs to Diamond Cross, and I don't care how long Dudley Stuart's stock has grazed on it. That don't make it his!"

The big fellow—Nate—smiled coldly and with his right hand pushed back his eager companion, who had started to crowd around him in order to get at the smaller one. "Let me get this straight, Snyder," Nate said, his voice ominous. "You callin' my boss a son of a bitch?"

Snyder suddenly moistened dry lips. "Not if he don't deserve it, Nate! But tarnation! If the shoe fits, he'll damn well have to wear it!"

"You heard him, Nate," said the milky-faced gunslick softly. "He just as much as called Dudley a son of a bitch."

"Let me handle this, Kid," said Nate. "I done heard him myself."

Nate said this to his companion without turning to face him. He was staring quietly, almost happily, down at Snyder now—the way a cobra was supposed to stare at its victim a moment before striking.

"Now, hold it, Nate," the small rancher cried, his voice filling the saloon with its unpleasant whine. "I ain't goin' to draw on you! And sure as hell not on that killer beside you!" With that he deliberately held both hands up and backed carefully away from the bar. "I got witness. You can't make me draw my weapon."

"Guess maybe I can't, at that," said Nate.

Before Snyder could pull his hands down to protect himself, Nate drew his six-gun and with meticulous brutality smashed its barrel across Snyder's face, opening a gash across the man's left cheekbone. The force of the blow sent Snyder reeling back. He thrust out one hand blindly. It came down on a table, tipping it. The rancher went down amidst a clatter of falling tables and shattering glasses. He struck the floor heavily and lay in the wreckage, only barely conscious.

Nate was evidently the kind whose rage feeds on itself. Striding closer to the prone man, he kicked him viciously in the side. He did it twice, measuring each kick carefully. With each measured blow, the man on the floor uttered a tiny, barely audible groan. It was perhaps because he craved a more dramatic response that Nate was goaded into a more vicious mood. Snatching up a chair, he was in the act of bringing it crashing down on the prostrate man's head when Zach's beer glass hit him on the side of his head.

The stein bounced high, the sound of it on Nate's skull sounding loud in the awed room. Nate's knees appeared to buckle. He staggered to one side, the chair dropping from hs hands. Barely conscious, he kept himself erect by hanging onto the bar with both hands.

Zach had left his table by then and was already striding swiftly toward Nate's companion. Before the Kid could bring up his six-gun, Zach reached out deftly and yanked the brim of his hat down over his eyes. Then, swiftly, he twisted the big gun out of the small hand and stuck it into his belt.

Nate, still clinging groggily to the bar, straightened himself and peered painfully over at Zach. He reached his hand up to the back of his head where Zach's stein had struck him.

"I'm armed now, Nate," Zach said. "I've got your partner's gun. You want to even scores?"

Sullenly, Nate shook his head. His little eyes were filled with hate; but there was a furtive wariness in them as well. He didn't know this stranger. Prudence told him he had better go slow until he did.

Seething, the Kid said, "Give me back my gun, mister. You got no right taking what's mine."

Zach lifted the Kid's revolver out of his belt. It was a gleaming, well-kept, ivory-handled Smith & Wesson .44, a double-action. He smiled and handed it back to the young man. "You keep it in that holster now, hear?"

Snatching the revolver from Zach, the Kid holstered it and then smiled. It was not a pleasant smile. "You'll get yours, mister. You got it coming. That's a promise." The voice was quiet, with the cold whisper of death in it.

"I don't like to be threatened, punk," Zach said.

He reached out swiftly, again snapped the Kid's hat brim down over his eyes, slapped him hard on one cheek, then backhanded him on the other. The Kid's head snapped around sharply each time. Before he could claw his gun out, Zach spun him around, planted his boot in the small of his back, then pushed. The Kid went stumbling out through the batwings, just missing the incoming town constable.

The lawman carried a shotgun. "All right, now," the fellow burst out. "What the hell's goin' on in here?"

"Nothing much, Wally!" someone from the back yelled. "This here stranger just bought into that feud between the Slash D and the Diamond Cross! Don't look like he'll be in this valley long!"

The crowd burst into laughter at that. Grinning slyly at the laughter, Nate walked past the town marshal, heading for the door. He glanced at Zach. "You heard the Kid, mister—and what that jasper back there just said. We'll tend to you soon enough. Just don't go thinkin' you can run out on us before we get a chance to settle up."

As Nate shouldered his way out of the saloon, Snyder, sitting up on the floor, his hand held up to his bleeding cheek, groaned. He was still too dazed to know what had happened after he had been struck down by Nate Claw. The town marshal walked over to Snyder and peered down at the injured man.

"You all right, Snyder?"

Snyder blinked his eyes a couple of times, then struggled to his feet. Nate's savage kicks into Snyder's side must have had an effect. The moment Snyder tried to stand upright, he groaned and clutched at his side.

"You all right?" the constable repeated.

Snyder swallowed painfully and nodded his head. "Sure, Wally. Sure. Just a little misunderstanding."

At once the patrons began drifting back to their games or the bar. The level of conversation rose steadily. The immediate excitement was over, but it was obvious these men would be chewing over what they had just witnessed for a long time to come.

Zach returned to his table. Somewhat groggily, Snyder followed him and slumped down, uninvited, at Zach's table. "I guess I should thank you," he managed, working his jaw painfully back and forth with his right hand.

The man sounded reluctant, as if thanking someone was an expression of weakness. Zach looked at Snyder for a long moment before replying. Then he spoke to the man softly. "Hell, Snyder, you don't have to do nothing if you don't want to. I didn't do that for your thanks, anyway. I just don't like horse killers, wife beaters, or bullies. But let me tell you something, mister. You don't have the sand to match your mouth. The next time them hombres get you in a corner, they likely won't let you out. I'd remember that if I were you."

Snyder pushed himself angrily to his feet. "Hey, now, I don't have to take that from you. I didn't ask for your help."

Zach sighed. "Snyder, I'm just trying to tell you to be careful. You and I are in this together. We're both fighting the same man, though maybe you didn't know that."

"No," Snyder said, still angry. "That's something I didn't know. And I'm not so sure I want you in this fight with me." With that, he turned on his heels and stalked from the saloon.

Zach leaned back in his chair and shook his head. As an ally, Snyder was not going to be very reliable. Perhaps he should not have been so hard on him—but Snyder seemed to be a man reckless beyond good sense, or at least beyond his capacity to withstand whatever retaliation his surly manner invited.

The girl who had served Nate his beer was approaching his table warily. He glanced up at her and smiled. "How about another beer?" he asked her. "I didn't get a chance to finish that last one."

She smiled warily. "Miss Jane would like to see you in her office, Mr. Stuart," she said. "She—told me to come get you as soon as the trouble died down."

"Ah," Zach said, pleased. "And just where might Jane's office be, ma'am?"

The girl pointed to a door at the other end of the bar.

Zach thanked her and got to his feet and started across the saloon toward the office. He had to skirt the barkeep and a swamper who were busy sweeping up the broken glass and righting the tables and chairs. He knocked softly on the door and it was immediately pulled open.

Jane Durrell was standing there, a pleased smile on her face. She was bigger than he had imagined her, much bigger, her cheeks round and rouged, her hair in faded ringlets hanging to her shoulder. Why was it, he thought unhappily, that old whores got so fat? As he remembered her, Jane had been so pretty it had caused an ache in him whenever she had lifted him in her arms or sat him on her lap.

"Come in, Zach," she said heartily, her voice heavier than he remembered it, almost masculine now in its rough assertiveness. "Does me good to see you!"

"Me, too, Jane," Zach said, a bit flustered. "You've got quite a place here."

Zach stepped into the office and Jane closed the door and turned to look at him, still beaming. Then she opened her arms. Zach stepped close and returned her warm bear hug, and suddenly the old memories flooded over him.

She stepped back to look at him again and shook her head in wonder. "You're a man now," she said. "Every inch." She smiled ruefully. "I could see the shock in your eyes, Zach. I'm no longer that slim young girl who used to read you to sleep and take you on picnics, am I."

"You're still Jane," Zach said, "the best friend my mother ever had, and the nicest playmate an adoring little roughneck could ever wish for. I had an impossible crush on you, Jane."

She smiled. This time it was the old Jane looking out at him, and he felt a sudden rush of affection. "I know, Zach," she said.

"Sorry about that scuffle out there. Two of Dudley's men had Snyder of the Diamond Cross in a corner. No permanent damage, though. Just a few broken glasses."

"I saw it, Zach. Thought it would be best if I kept out of it. You seemed to be handling things nicely. And you were going to have to introduce yourself to Nate Claw and the Kid sooner or later."

Zach nodded grimly. "I wasn't much impressed with Snyder."

"I didn't think you would be," Jane responded, walking over to her private bar in the corner. "But he's got the biggest spread beside yours. You'll need his cooperation."

Zach slumped into an old leather armchair while Jane built them both drinks. The office was functional, as businesslike and efficient in its decorations and furnishings as was this new, older Jane Durrell.

He still was having some difficulty separating in his mind this older, buxom woman from that slim, vivacious girl Zach had known as a child—one of Miss Helen's most prized attractions. Before Miss Helen and Zach's mother had left for Texas, Jane had been his nurse and companion. Zach still remembered vividly the summer days when Jane would take him on long rides into the surrounding country, using Helen's buggy and always packing a huge picnic lunch. On many of these excursions, Zach's mother, suitably bundled and hidden away in folds of blankets, would accompany them as they drove back across the tracks and through the town—Jane and Zach keyed to a nervous pitch as they kept Zach's mother from being recognized. During those five years that Zach and his mother lived at Miss Helen's Parlor House, Miss Helen had been able to make stick her refusal to allow Dudley Stuart or any of his riders to frequent her "parlor house." The result was that Dudley Stuart never knew that his wife had lived or that she had given birth to his son; it was a secret the doctor who delivered Zach and the girls of the house willingly kept from the owner of the Slash D. But at last the deception had become too difficult to maintain, and Helen sold out to Jane and took Zach and his mother to Texas with her.

"Best Scotch west of Denver," Jane said, handing Zach his drink.

Zach took it. "Thanks."

"I've got the deeds," Jane said. "Over at my desk. There's a map, too."

Zach hauled himself to his feet and walked over to Jane's flattop desk. Jane went around behind it, pulled open a deep drawer, and took from it a large shoe box, which she sat on the desk. Zach was not wrong in detecting a small, triumphant smile on her face. He did not blame her. For close to five years they had been building toward this moment.

Zach opened the box and pulled from it twelve deeds, each one of which gave him title to land that Dudley Stuart had always considered his own by right of possession. Hefty bribes to the clerk at the land office had kept each purchase a secret from Dudley Stuart, or any who might want to apprise him of the purchases. Fortunately, the Slash D owner and his riders were not the most highly favored citizens of this valley. There were few who would go out of their way to help the man or his surly crew.

The precaution, however, had been a wise one. Each year Jane had sent Zach one or two, sometimes three, deeds to sign, each parcel of land contiguous with the previous parcel in a crazy checkerboard that now effectively encircled Slash D, with Jane Durrell's own ranch, the partially abandoned Flying T, as its base. Years before, she had taken the small ranch in payment for a bad debt. Only occasionally did she visit the ranch, usually on hot summer days when she would take a wagon load of her girls out there—as much to remind Dudley Stuart and the rest of the valley who owned the ranch as to give her girls a needed respite from the smoke-filled masculine world in which they toiled.

As Zach looked over the deeds, Jane took from her upper desk drawer the deed to the Flying T itself. "Here it is, Zach, all legal and proper, each land parcel added on, all of it signed over to you for the sum of two thousand dollars. Your receipt for that amount is clipped to the deed."

Zach took up the deed, noted the receipt, smiled over at Jane, then tucked the deed into his frock coat's inside pocket. "Jane," he began, "you know how I'd like to thank you for all you've—"

"Stow it," Jane interrupted gruffly. "I'm doing this for myself and for Helen as well as for your poor mother—just as much as I am doing it for you. It is up to you now, Zach. The time has come—as you told me so often in your letters—for Dudley Stuart to pay the piper."

Zach nodded grimly, then glanced back to Jane's desk. "Is that the map you wrote me about?" he asked, pointing to a clumsily folded map.

"Yes," she said. "Let me show it to you."

She quickly unfolded it, cleared off the desk, and spread out the map.

"Looks like you spent a lot of time on it," Zach said, impressed.

"I did, Zach. The mornings, usually, while the girls were sleeping and the saloon was being swamped out. I looked forward to working on it."

Zach's Flying T land holdings were outlined in red crayon. The boundaries of the Slash D were in green. Dave Snyder's Diamond Cross—a shade smaller in overall acreage than Zach's and the ranch that effectively hemmed in the Slash D to the north—was outlined in blue. The smaller outfits that clustered to the west of the Slash D were traced in black crayon.

It was obvious at a glance that with Zach's Flying T and Snyder's Diamond Cross as barriers, the only direct access to fresh water that Dudley had was to the south, where he had a generous stretch of the Little Whiskey to rely on, and in Indian Springs to the north. The other water holes and creeks he now counted on to take care of his vast herds would be completely cut off by Zach's

Flying T. His cattle would have to cross Zach's land, or, failing that, cut across Diamond Cross or one of the smaller ranches.

Many of these water holes and creeks were, in fact, legal Slash D holdings, and each one Jane had meticulously shaded a light green. But Dudley's problem now was that he no longer had access to them, since he had neglected to file claim on those lands between—land that now belonged to Zach's Flying T.

Zach straightened and nodded, pleased, as he continued to look down at the map. The Slash D was now a mere shadow of its former self, a thin wedge of land extending south to the Little Whiskey, with a broad, but shortened, arm of land stretching northwest to Indian Springs. On such reduced holdings, the Slash D could not hope to graze the sizable herds it was now handling. It would have to pull its horns in, become just one more cattle outfit in the valley.

And that was something that Zach knew his father would never do.

"We've done it, Jane," Zach said, picking up his drink and stepping away from the desk. "Let me have that map. I'll put it on the wall in my bedroom at the ranch. It is something I will want to study and consult—often."

"That's what I thought," Jane said with a smile.

As Jane refolded the map, Zach walked over to the window and looked out at Canyon City's Main Street. He could see across to another saloon, a general store, and a bank on the corner. Except for the sound of the rain, the town was eerily quiet. Horses slogged along silently, the clop of their hooves and the rumble of wagon wheels muffled by the gumbolike mud. The few men Zach glimpsed running through the puddles and pounding along the wooden walks made hardly a sound on the soggy wooden planking. There was just the monotonous pounding of the rain slanting almost straight down.

He turned to look back at Jane. "I met Skelkins at the

station when he took the casket. He said we have three days yet before the burial."

Jane nodded. "That should give us plenty of time. I've already sent the telegrams. There are two surviving sisters and a brother. Both your mother's parents have been deceased for some time."

Zach turned back to the window. He hoped it was not raining when they buried his mother. But if it was, it would be fitting—after the life she had lived since that night when Dudley flung her from him with such destructive, crippling brutality.

That was why Zach had returned, to seek out and ruin—to destroy completely—the man who had done that to his mother. It made no difference that Dudley Stuart was his father.

He would destroy him anyway.

Two

STILL TALL IN THE saddle despite his sixty-three years, Dudley Stuart rode into the Slash D compound a little before noon the next day at the head of a sullen, bedraggled crew of thoroughly wet cowpokes.

It was still raining. The rain was not slanting down as heavily as in the last three days; but it was enough to creep in under the collars of the men's slickers and trickle coldly down their backs until it soaked their shirts and gathered in an icy, sodden mass just above the snug gunbelts they all wore. Still, as Dudley knew well enough, they needed this rain. His men would just have to put up with the wet camps, the chill, damp bedrolls, the clammy feel of their boots, and the bone-deep cold that seemed to have settled in. Hell, in his day he'd had to live through far worse than this on those long trail drives north from Texas. Why, these men didn't know what real privation was.

Dudley kept ahead of his men and pointed his black at the horse stable, offering no conversation to his crew. Dismounting in front of the stable, he gave the black to Silas, who stepped out into the rain to take the black's bridle and lead him into the barn. The wrangler had been nipping on his moonshine, Dudley realized, catching a strong whiff of the old man's breath. The wrangler's sullenness and the red gleam in his eyes were simply further indications to Dudley that the wrangler's drinking might be getting out of hand. But he had no desire to tangle with the old reprobate now.

Dudley strode across the compound through the bedraggled ranks of riders now approaching the stable. He said not a word to any of them and not a hand spoke to him as they rode past. Dudley's long, curly hair was snow white. His handlebar mustache was yellowing, and the beetling brows were gray. But his dark eyes still looked out at the world with a bleak, uncompromising resolve. His riders called him the Old Man among themselves, Dudley knew. They did not like him. They all respected and feared him, though, and this was all Dudley wanted. Respect was something you could see harden and grow sharper with the years. It was something you could build on. Love and affection were useless, treacherous feelings that always seemed to putrify into something mean and undependable.

Nate Claw was standing on the porch in front of the ranch office, close in under the roof's overhang to keep himself out of the rain. The Kid was standing beside him. They straightened themselves a little as Dudley drew closer. Dudley noticed this and was pleased. Lately, he had wondered if the Kid might not be getting a mite too big for his britches.

"What's up, Nate?" Dudley asked as he strode past them into his office.

As they followed him in, he shrugged out of his yellow slicker and hung it on a peg beside the door. His heavy, broadcloth shirt was soaked about the shoulders and his boots were sodden, but he paid no heed to this as he strode around behind his desk and slacked his large, still well proportioned body back into his swivel-chair.

"Well, damn it, Nate," Dudley barked, as he reached into a drawer for his whiskey. "Out with it! Did you let Snyder whip your ass? Or did his old lady chase you fellows off his place with a broom?"

"That ain't what happened at all, Mr. Stuart," Nate

explained hastily. "I tried to shivy Snyder in the Belle Fourche, where we caught up to him, and I had the poor stupid son of bitch right where I wanted him when this dude interfered."

"Dude?"

"That's how he was dressed, anyway. He just got into town, I heard."

"What's his name?"

"I don't know, Mr. Stuart. But he made the two of us look pretty damn silly. He kept me from finishing off Snyder and booted the Kid out of the Belle Fourche."

Dudley looked at the Kid. The young man was still standing by the doorway, his cold, lidded eyes almost reptilian. At Nate's words, his face had grown pinched, hard. In the dim, rainy light that filtered in through the window, the Kid's face reminded Dudley of a bleached skull. "Booted you out of the saloon, did he, Kid?"

The Kid compressed his lips angrily. He was seething at the memory of what had happened. Then he replied, his voice tight with rage. "This here dude caught Nate on the back of his head with a beer stein, Mr. Stuart. He knocked *Nate* plumb silly."

Dudley looked back at Nate. This man was his foreman. It was bad for anyone—for any reason—to get the best of a Slash D rider. It was downright dangerous if it happened to the Slash D's foreman and his *segundo*. "Seems to me, Nate, this fellow doesn't have proper respect for the Slash D. You think he's a hired gun? You think maybe Snyder brought him up to put backbone into that damned association of theirs?"

"Didn't look like it. This dude waited an awful long time before making his move."

Dudley nodded. "I see. Just someone buying into a quarrel. That's how you see it?"

Nate smiled uncertainly. "I wouldn't know, Mr. Stuart. But he did stick his nose in, that's for sure."

"Well, I expect the next time you meet this dude, you'll cut him down a peg. I assume you know how to do that?"

Both men nodded quickly.

"Good! See that it is done soon enough so that people forget what happened in the Belle Fourche. Do you men understand?"

Again they nodded. Dudley lifted out two more glasses, cleaned the dust out with his right thumb, and placed them down on the desk blotter beside his own glass.

"It'll take the chill out of your bones," he told them as he poured three stiff belts. "Drink up. Then go see to that fellow."

"We'll get that son of a bitch, Mr. Stuart," promised Nate, as he reached for his glass.

"I know you will," Dudley said, smiling coldly.

The three men drank without a toast—silently, grimly. Dudley was reaching for the bottle when he heard someone running through the rain. He looked toward the door just as it swung open. One of his hands, Crowley, leaned in.

"A lone rider's comin'!" he told Dudley.

"Thank you, Crowley," Dudley said, getting to his feet. "From what direction?"

"South."

"From Canyon City, then."

Dudley was curious. Who the hell would be riding to the Slash D through this downpour—all the way from Canyon City? Dudley moved past Nate and the Kid and stepped out onto the porch.

The rider was past the stable now, his face—peering out from under his dripping black Stetson—growing steadily clearer. Nate, standing close beside him, gasped suddenly.

"That's *him!* That's the one, Mr. Stuart. I'd recognize that face anywhere! That's the dude we told you about!"

"Well, now," Dudley remarked, frowning, "he's sure as hell making it easy for us. You *sure* that's the one? It don't make much sense for him to come riding in here like this, after what you two just told me."

"That's him, all right," said the Kid ominously. "Just let me take him, Mr. Dudley." He drew his Smith & Wesson.

"Now just steady down, Kid," Dudley said, "and put that gun away."

Dudley felt uneasy. There had to be more to this than what Nate had told him. Who the hell was this lone rider? After what he had done to Nate and the Kid, how could he be fool enough to ride out here all alone like this?

The rider was now halfway between the ranchhouse and the stable. Dudley saw him glance swiftly to his right as he took in the unfinished house back among the cottonwoods.

The stranger's swift glance alerted Dudley—brought alive a long-dead memory. He looked more closely at the rider's features. Something deep within him came alive, and with it the aching regret—that old, old ache he knew he could never shake. It had something to do with the shape of the stranger's face, the set to his jaw, the way he carried himself erect as he rode. Against his better judgment—against all good sense—Dudley found himself thinking of Theresa.

Zach's glance confirmed what he had surmised when he first rode into the ranch. A large, almost palatial, two-story mansion seemed to be under construction deep within the grove of cottonwoods beside the ranchhouse. Scaffolding still clung to one wall. Yet nothing about the building was new. The shingles had long since peeled off, the unpainted clapboard siding was warped and cracking from years of exposure to the elements, the windows were all out, the large chimney remained unfinished; there were gaping holes just before the chimney, where construction had been halted, revealing studs and the raw unpainted interior.

The big unfinished house spoke with sad eloquence of shattered dreams, of the futility of hope—and of the inevitability of death and decay.

Zach swung his gaze back to Dudley Stuart, ignoring the other two standing beside him. There was no doubt in his mind that this was his father, the man he had ridden out to see—and to invite to a funeral.

As he neared the porch, Zach saw Slash D hands hurrying across the muddy compound through the rain, some streaming from the bunkhouse, others from the barns. He paid them no heed as he pulled his mount to a halt, his gaze fixed on the tall rancher standing on the porch.

The man looked vaguely familiar. Zach had, of course, met him before. In his own mirror. It was from this stranger's loins that he had sprung, after all. This man was his father. Though Zach should have felt some faint stirrings of kinship, all he felt was anger. Feeling the man's implacable eyes burning at him through the pelting rain, he remembered his mother's suffering, the years she had spent in a wheelchair, the pain she had been forced to endure the last years before her death—the result, her physicians insisted, of an injury to her spine incurred many years before, on a dark night when she had been flung from her husband's horse.

A remote, calculating fury steadied Zach as he said, "I have come to invite you to a funeral, Dudley."

The rancher was confused. "What are you trying to tell me, mister? Who the hell are you, anyway?"

"I meant what I said, Dudley. I would like you to attend a funeral. To pay your last respects and all." By that time Dudley Stuart's riders had gathered in a large semicircle around Zach.

Dudley was angry now. "Speak plain, mister. Whose funeral?"

"The funeral," Zach told him, "is for my mother, Theresa Stuart."

Dudley flinched visibly, almost as if Zach had struck him across the face. Then he was himself again, only the sudden pallor of his face revealing what he had felt in that instant. "Who put you up to this, mister? And who the hell are you, anyway?"

"I'm your son, Dudley. Zach Stuart."

"That's impossible! My wife's dead. I never had a son! You're plumb loco, mister! Now, who put you up to this?"

Zach leaned closer to Dudley. "My mother wasn't dead when you flung her from your horse that night, Dudley. And she didn't die later, when she might have. It would have been kinder for both of us if she had." Zach straightened in his saddle. "Like I just told you. I rode out here through the rain to invite you to your wife's funeral. It will be at the Rose Hill Cemetery just outside town, tomorrow morning at ten."

Zach touched the brim of his hat lightly, then pulled his horse around and rode back through the silent ranks of ranch hands and on across the compound. As he left it, he turned in his saddle. Through the slanting rain he could see that Dudley Stuart was still standing on the porch, looking after him. But he seemed to have shrunken noticeably in size.

Zach smiled grimly, turned back around in his saddle, and rode on through the chill rain.

Three

DUDLEY STUART WAS SITTING in his big armchair, staring out at the dark night, when he heard the door to his bedroom open.

He turned his head, startled. It was Felicia, his old housekeeper. She had been sharing his bed for the past fifteen years.

"I don't want you tonight," he told her. He looked back at the window and the night. "Not tonight, Felicia."

The woman was as tall as Dudley; despite her age, her face was still handsome. She had large, soft, warm eyes. Felicia had combed her hair out and was dressed simply in a long white nightgown. She had not visited Dudley's bed for some time now and was surprised at his refusal. But her dark face revealed nothing of what she felt. Without a word, she turned and left the room.

Dudley did not hear the door close, just as he no longer heard the rain pounding on the roof or saw the black night yawning before him. . . .

It was twenty-five years earlier, and Dudley was sitting in the same bedroom, finishing a whiskey—and with it the bottle. But it had done him no good, no good at all. He pushed himself to his feet and left the bedroom, aware that he was moving somewhat unsteadily. He stood in the living room, swaying slightly.

Where was she? Sweet Jesus, how he needed her! To love a woman like this—to hunger after her in this way—was the sharpest pain he had ever experienced; it was a serpent's tooth embedded in his heart. It was monstrous, demeaning, undignified! Oh, God, why did she not come?

But he didn't have to ask God. He knew where she was, where she always was lately: sucking around that greenhorn they'd taken on this spring—a mewling milksop not yet dry behind the ears. He was still writing letters home to his mother! Only the stupid son of a bitch couldn't write.

Or so he said.

Aghast, he stood stock-still for a moment, rage igniting him with a suddenness that made his head speed. How could he not have seen this sooner?

Groaning, he flung himself out into the night and headed for the bunkhouse, the hot spring night fanning his rage into a mindless fury. The milksop bunked in the small addition to the rear of the bunkhouse. Silas, the wrangler, shared the small room with him, but—unlike the milksop—spent most of his time with the older hands in the main bunkhouse when he wasn't in the stables caring for the horses.

So they were usually alone, then. Of course! A kaleidoscope of tormenting images rose before Dudley's eyes. Theresa alone with the young cowpoke in the bunkhouse. The lamp low. Her young body comforting his. Her sweet cry as he pleased her. Yes! And this despite her protests to her husband that she was too far along in her pregnancy to support his weight. The wanton!

Reaching the corner of the bunkhouse, he saw the dim glow of a lamp in the rear room. He pulled up, suddenly bewildered. He did not want to find them together. It would be too fearsome. Shuddering, he contemplated the black heart of woman. As the Bible proclaimed, she was forever the Strange Woman, her mouth sweeter than oil, her end bitter as wormwood and sharp as a two-edged sword, her steps taking hold on hell!

He could hear them! Hesitating no longer, he rushed to the door, flung his shoulder against it, and burst it open. The door slammed back against one of the bunks.

In the light from that single, damning lamp he saw that all was just as he had envisioned it—Theresa with her arms about the cowpoke, the tangle of her thick auburn curls caressing the milksop's pale, moonstruck face. At his entry they swung their faces toward him, guilt and terror writ large on their adulterous faces. Behind him, Dudley heard someone enter the bunkhouse. A restraining hand grabbed at his arm. He pulled free of it as easily as if he had been brushing through a cobweb and advanced on the cowering lovers.

"Dudley!" Theresa cried, jumping to her feet, overturning the small table that he now saw was between them.

A pen rolled along the floor and he was dimly aware of an inkwell spilling a black puddle before it as it rolled after the pen. He paid no attention as he swung the back of his hand, catching Theresa on the side of her face and flinging her violently backward. The back of her knees struck the bunk and her torso swung back, her head crunching cruelly against the wall. Only partly conscious, she rolled slackly off the bunk and sprawled facedown on the wooden floor.

The cowpoke had scrambled to the rear of his bunk and was in the act of pulling an enormous revolver from its holster. But the moment the weapon was free, Dudley snatched it. He watched himself, as if from a great distance, as he turned the revolver quickly about, cocked it, and fired three times into the young man. With a cold, detached pleasure, Dudley watched the boy's astonished face as he slammed back against the wall, his hands held out uselessly to ward off further rounds. Slowly the cowpoke sagged to the floor, his eyes still wide, his face the color of the bedsheet he had snatched loose as he clutched at his bunk.

Dudley turned and with quick, furious strides reached Theresa's side. She was conscious now and turning to stare, speechless with terror, up at him. He flung the revolver, reached down, grabbed her thick hair, and began to drag her from the place. Silas was at the door. Dudley heard the man's protesting words but paid no heed as he brushed past him out into the hot night, still dragging his wife. As he neared the stable, he saw the crowd of punchers in front of the bunkhouse, watching. He snarled an order at them, and they hastily crowded back into the bunkhouse.

Inside the stable, he found his horsewhip. He dropped Theresa in the middle of the floor and unwound the long whip. She had been moaning softly all during the time Dudley had been dragging her behind him. Now, suddenly, she began to weep piteously. He heard her calling to him, her voice broken.

"You shouldn't have, Dudley! The poor boy! Oh, that poor boy! You killed him!"

"Crying for your lover, are you!" he shouted, his voice resonant with justified rage. "Then I'll send you after him!"

His whip snaked out, its tip licking at her back, stinging her frightfully. She recoiled from it. He sent the whip at her again. This time it wrapped itself with a nasty crack around her shoulder. When he pulled it free, flesh and part of her bodice came with it. She screamed. No longer was she calling for her lover. He sent the whip at her, this time catching her about the arm.

Still watching it all as if from a vast distance, he horsewhipped her with a precision that made himself proud, keeping at it until the woman at last gave up trying to crawl away from the remorseless lash. Slowly, he folded the whip and approached her. She was still conscious.

"You beast!" she cried hoarsely. "You killed an innocent boy! And now you are going to kill me—and your unborn child! To think I loved you! How could I have *ever* loved you?"

Her words lacerated. They were not what he had expected. She should have been contrite, begging for mercy, for forgiveness—for her life! He struck her repeatedly about her face and neck with the handle of his whip.

"Beast," she gasped weakly when he had done. "Hateful beast—"

He dropped the whip and took her neck in his huge hands and began to squeeze. He would shut her up somehow. Her eyes began to protrude grotesquely. She beat upon him weakly.

Something struck him hard from behind, momentarily stunning him. Control returned. He released Theresa, saw her head strike the floor. Turning, he saw who it was who had struck him. Young Silas, the wrangler. The fellow took a step backward, but his face was defiant, his eyes blazing with anger.

"You've killed her!" Silas cried.

Dudley looked back down at Theresa. She was lying as still as death, her head resting on the floor, her face turned to one side away from him. He was glad. He did not want to look upon those bulging eyes again. Backing away from her, he glanced swiftly at Silas.

"Saddle my horse—then take care of the other one. Do you understand?"

Silas nodded grimly and vanished out the door. Dudley looked back down at Theresa. He felt nothing. He knew what he had done now—saw clearly in that instant the awful threshhold over which he had just stepped. Looking at the pitifully still figure crumpled on the barn floor before him, he was able to recreate in his mind's eye his every monstrous act from the moment he burst into the bunkhouse until Silas struck him from behind. He knew he should feel sorrow—anguish, certainly—but he felt nothing. He was dead inside. He would never feel anything again. Not love. Not hate. Nothing.

And this woman lying dead in front of him had done this, this Strange Woman, this adulteress . . . !

Dudley pulled his gaze away from the rain-streaked window panes and rested his face in his hands. If only it had ended that night. But that had been only the beginning of his torment. With an almost audible groan, Dudley got to his feet and began to pace the bedroom, a demented beast pacing the cage of his past. . . .

When he returned from Canyon City that night, he found that Silas had alredy buried the boy along with all his personal effects somewhere in the hills, leaving no trace of him in that bunkhouse room—except, of course, for the blood that had soaked into the rough-hewn timber of the floorboards.

Soon thereafter his riders began drifting off, taking other employment on distant ranches. They would appear before him in small groups of three or four, rarely singly, asking for their time. They would offer no excuse and Dudley would ask none. He knew why they could not remain Slash D riders. They knew what he had done and what ghosts now prowled this suddenly forlorn ranch. Each day as they rode into the compound, they saw the unfinished abandoned house that was to have been Dudley and Theresa's new home. It was for them—as it was for Dudley—a constant reminder of what this ranch had lost—and of what Dudley had done.

Dudley hired new hands and looked for toughness in them above everything else. They had to be as tough and as uncompromising as he was, for what he had done he had had to do. He was pleased that Silas stayed on, though he was startled to see the young man's greater and greater dependence on the bottle. It seemed that he too had his ghosts to exorcise. Dudley understood and did not complain.

His foreman, Mike Dodds, was the last of his old hands

to leave. When Mike entered Dudley's office that afternoon, the spring roundup completed, the new hands welded into as efficient a band as the crew that had left, Dudley had been about to offer Dodds a sizable raise in pay. He had even considered someday making him a full partner.

"Sorry to hear you're leaving, Mike," Dudley said, not trying to conceal his disappointment.

The tall, lean cowhand moved uncomfortably before Dudley's gaze. "Thank you, Mr. Stuart. But I reckon I'll be riding out soon's you can give me my time. My gear's all stowed."

"Take any horse in the string," Dudley told him. "Any one that suits your fancy. That big paint you favor, if you've a mind."

"Thank you, Mr. Stuart."

Dudley had his cash box already out. He counted out the man's wages, then added a small bonus. As Mike thanked him for the bonus and carefully picked the silver coins up off the desk and dropped them into his saddlebag, Dudley leaned back in his chair and studied the man's face a moment. He had not tried to convince any of the other men to stay. But this man he needed. This man he felt he could trust, and he had to have someone like that around him.

"Why are you leaving, Mike?" Dudley asked abruptly. "I thought I could count on you to understand."

"Understand?"

"Why I had to do what I did—that night. You stuck by me. You've remained loyal, and I assumed it was because you realized that I did what I had to do, that I had no recourse."

"You think that's why I stayed?"

"Isn't it?"

"No, Mr. Stuart, it isn't. I stayed on because you needed me to lick this new crew into shape."

Dudley smiled thinly. "And now you're going."

"Yes." The tall fellow slung the saddlebag over his

shoulder and fixed his now cold eyes on Dudley. He hesitated only a moment. "You made a mistake that night, Mr. Stuart. You killed an innocent young cowboy and lost a woman who loved only you."

Dudley dropped both his hands down flat upon the desk. He would hear no more of this; he was sorry he had brought the matter up. "Now, you listen here, Dodds!"

But the man kept on remorselessly: "That young feller got a letter that day. You remember. I brought the mail in from Canyon City myself. The letter was from an uncle of the boy's. I read it to him. His mother had just died. The boy had been writing to her at least once a week—with your wife's kind help—because he knew just how sick his mother was. But when he got that letter from his uncle, it pretty near did him in. We tried to quiet him, but he asked for your wife to comfort him.

"So I went after her. It was late, but she said she knew you would understand. She was like a mother to that young cowpoke, Mr. Stuart. The poor fellow wasn't more'n sixteen or seventeen, not yet dry behind the ears. He wasn't no threat to you, Mr. Stuart, no more than I was or any of them hands. We all respected your wife. She was good to all of us and kind and always willing to help. So I guess I been feelin' pretty low over what happened, especially since I was the one that came to fetch her that night. But like I said, she assured me that you would understand. Only you didn't. You didn't understand at all."

Dudley tried to say something. But no words would come. He felt as if a massive dose of poison had just been injected into his bloodstream. He was paralyzed. A sick ache spread through every cell of his body, penetrating even into his bones.

Mike Dodds tugged his hat down securely. "Goodbye, Mr. Stuart. You don't have to believe me if you don't want—and maybe it would be a lot better for you if you didn't. Only thing is, I didn't want to ride out of here with you thinking I understood why you did what you did. Because I don't. I never will."

Dodds spun on his heels then, ducked his head, and disappeared out the door....

Dudley stopped his pacing, his wide eyes staring into a corner of his room. After all these years, he could still hear that foreman's words: *You killed an innocent young cowboy and lost a woman who loved only you.*

And then Dudley saw again the figure of his son riding toward him through the rain, his face implacable, his eyes burning with hatred. His son! Tall in the saddle! And as fierce and terrible in his wrath as his father. The thought smote him like a fist. His hands dropped to his side. He tipped his head back. Bursting from his throat came a cry of baffled rage and terror—the awesome scream of a human soul twisting now in the everlasting embrace of hell's fire.

Almost asleep in her small room off the kitchen, Felicia sat up in bed, startled. She knew what she had heard, and it sent an icy shiver of fear racing up her spine. Flinging back the covers, she found her slippers, lit the lamp on the nightstand, then hurried down the hall to Dudley's room. She pushed it open and peered cautiously in, her heart pounding with alarm.

Dudley was standing by the window, still peering out at the black night. He did not turn at the sound of her entrance.

"It's all right, Felicia," he said, his voice unintentionally harsh. "I did not mean to wake you. Go back to bed. Early tomorrow morning I will want you to press my black worsted suit." He turned to face her then, and in the dim light from the single lamp on his dresser, she saw the face of a man who must have just witnessed terrible things. She took an involuntary step back.

"I am going to a funeral." he told her.

Four

ZACH WAS HAVING DIFFICULTY hearing the youthful minister. The man's voice was high and thin; the rain and gusting wind kept carrying his words away. As Zach kept his hand on the brim of his hat, he managed to hear that part about ashes to ashes and dust to dust. He saw the minister step back and nod to the gravediggers. The coffin was lowered. The minister looked over at Zach. Zach left Jane's side and dropped the first clod of mud onto the ebony coffin, then stepped back.

Behind him, Jane was weeping softly now. Theresa's two sisters and brother were standing in a group apart from Zach and Jane. They had made it abundantly clear from the moment of their arrival in Canyon City what they thought of their sister's friendship with a madam and saloon keeper. Yet they had come to pay their last respects, and that was all Zach had expected of them.

Jane, wiping her eyes, moved up beside Zach. "That sonofabitch," she said softly. "He didn't show."

The sound of hooves on the soft ground below came to them. Turning, Zach glanced down the rain-swept slope and saw Dudley Stuart—his foreman and the Kid alongside him—leaving the road and riding through the cemetery gate and up the slope toward them.

One of his mother's sisters, a very old woman, an umbrella clutched in her bony hand, moved quickly over to Zach. She had a small, pinched face with bright, gimlet eyes. Ignoring Jane, she spoke excitedly to Zach.

"That's him! That's her husband! I remember the man!"

Zach turned to her. "Yes."

"And that's *your* father!"

"Yes."

The other sister hurried over then, the brother also, all three of them watching Dudley's approach with a venomous fascination, like smaller birds of prey watching a real vulture swoop down.

Above the rain's steady drizzle, the sound of shovels slicing into the wet dirt, followed by the thump of the heavy soil striking the coffin, came clearly to Zach. He moved with Jane away from the sound, the two sisters and the single wizened old man keeping close by him. The old man had disdained an umbrella, relying on his black, wide-brimmed hat to keep off the rain. His black suit was shiny in the rain, its contours plastered to the man's narrow shoulders and thin arms. His nose looked red, his face bleak in the chill rain.

Dudley pulled his horse to a halt beside them and looked down at the small party of mourners. He was dressed in black, the brim of his wide hat pulled down to protect his neck from the rain. The old rancher's face was heavily lined, his cheeks sunken. The light in his eyes softened somewhat as he glanced for a moment past Zach at the gravediggers shoveling the dirt into the grave.

"I'm late," Dudley said, looked back down at Zach. "I'm sorry."

"I had not expected you to show up," said Zach.

"Didn't figure you did. You just wanted this old man to realize what he had done. Ain't that right, son? You'd like Dudley Stuart to roast in the coals of hell some more."

"That's about it," Zach admitted.

"I see no tears in your eyes, son."

"And where the hell are yours?"

Dudley looked beyond Zach at Jane. "Miss Helen

never told me Theresa was alive—or that she had given birth to my son. That was wrong, Jane. And you took part in keeping that information from me all these years. That was a mean, spiteful thing to do."

"Yes," Jane replied shortly, her face cold. "But it gave me a certain satisfaction."

Dudley frowned and looked back at Zach. "Would it do any good for me to tell you how sorry I am, son? I made a mistake. A terrible mistake."

"No, it wouldn't do you any good, Dudley. And I'll thank you not to address me as your son again. I am no son of yours."

"You can deny me if you want, but I can't deny you. You favor your mother—and me. I saw that the moment I laid eyes on you yesterday."

"That's something I can't help, Dudley." Zach smiled thinly. "But I am sure there will come a day when you'll find no difficulty denying me."

"You're going to make me pay. Is that it?"

Zach smiled coldly up at his father. "Don't you think you've got it coming?"

"I've paid. I'm still paying. There's nothing you can say—no curse too awful—that I haven't hurled at myself. There's nothing you can do to me, Zach. I'm already a dead man."

"Not yet, you ain't. You still got your land, and the power that goes with that. You still got your health. You still get up in the morning and busy yourself with your empire of cattle and men and find some comfort in that."

"And you're going to take all that from me, are you?"

"I'm putting you on notice here—my mother's graveside. The last years of her life were filled with pain. You made her a cripple. When at last she said goodbye to me, it was a blessing. Dudley, I want you to feel what *she* felt."

Dudley straightened in his saddle and looked down at Zach with surprising intensity. At Zach's words, there had come over the man a transformation of a sort. A strength and vitality flowed back into his face. His powerful, craggy brows gave his face a fierce, almost ennobling power.

"Look at me, Zach. You see before you the ruin of a man. Take care you don't duplicate this ruin in yourself."

"There's too much hate in me for care, Dudley. I reckon that's the part of me that belongs to you, at that."

Zach's reply seemed to strike deep within Dudley. The rancher almost flinched. He said no more and turned his glance on the two men who had sat their horses patiently behind him. With a wave of his hand, he set them in motion. They turned their horses about and rode back down the slope. Dudley rode after them without looking back.

Zach turned to his mother's sisters and brother and thanked them for coming. They looked up at him with something approaching awe. They had heard him and knew what he intended. The oldest sister, the one who held the umbrella, leaned close. Reaching out with a thin, clawlike hand, she clutched him about the wrist.

"You must let this all pass now, my boy," she said, her voice high, querulous. "Forget that terrible man. Theresa is gone now; she is with God. Let that be an end to it."

Zach patted her hand, but did not reply. And when she tried to look into his eyes, he looked away. With a sigh, she turned from Zach, took her other sister by the arm and led her back down the path toward the surrey they had rented. The brother moved closer to Zach then, his narrow, pinched face searching Zach's hungrily.

"You'll fix him, won't you, boy!" he said hopefully. "I heard you and I think you can do it. You can stand up to that man. He ruined Theresa's life! I tried to tell her not to marry that man, but she would not listen to me. And she wouldn't listen to her father, neither." He shook his head bitterly. "She loved him, she told us. *Loved* that man!"

Shaking his head at the incomprehensibility of such a

thing, the old man bent himself away from Zach and, trembling like a branch in the wind, moved slowly down the path after his sisters.

Zach turned to Jane. Her umbrella tugged in the wind, hovering over their heads like a dark wing. A black bonnet enclosed her pale, round face. She wore a long, dark silk dress under her coat. She was no longer crying.

"Get those carpenters busy, Jane," Zach told her. "I'll be riding out now to meet the herd. Bill Handler should arrive tomorrow. I'd appreciate it if you would give him all the help you can in getting himself set at the ranch." Zach smiled grimly. "There'll be a load of barbed wire on that train with him."

Jane nodded. "I'll do all I can, Zach."

"You've already done more than any man could ask, Jane. From here on in, I'm figuring it's going to get pretty dangerous for you. Dudley will know pretty damn soon what your part in all this has been."

"That's only what I want, Zach." She reached out and took his arm, squeezing it tightly. "Do you know how long I have waited for this day? If only Miss Helen could be here beside me to see it. But I know," she went on fiercely, "that if there's a God in heaven, your mother's looking down right now."

Zach glanced away from Jane's fierce gaze. "Well, then, you just be careful, that's all. I won't be long. I should be back in less than a fortnight."

"Don't you worry about me none, Zach. You just do what you have to."

Zach patted Jane's arm. Together they walked down the slope toward their waiting carriage. Ahead of them, the old man was climbing carefully into the surrey beside his sisters. It was a sad day for the three of them, and Zach thought that perhaps he should not have asked Jane to invite them to the funeral—just buried his mother with himself and Jane in attendance. Perhaps. It was difficult, all of a sudden, to know for sure what the right thing was.

He thought he had known without a doubt what his course must be and nothing, even now, could persuade him to abandon that course.

But the words of his father were not easily dismissed: *You see before you the ruin of a man. Take care you don't duplicate this ruin in yourself.*

Five

ZACH HAD LEFT THE herd and stopped in Canyon City to check out a few matters with Jane—and to make sure she was all right—before continuing on to the Flying T. Manny Garcia and the two other hands he had signed on in Winchester had driven the five hundred head on to the ranch ahead of him; now, as Zach crested the gentle slope and looked down at his ranch, he saw that his men were already hard at work.

Most of the cattle had spilled into the meadow west of the ranchhouse and the larger flat beyond, while Garcia and the others worked on the small bunches they had driven into a corral behind the horse barn. From there they were driven one at a time into a smaller corral, where they were roped, thrown, their old brands vented, and a Flying T branded on the left hip with a running iron. The men were working doggedly and did not appear to notice Zach as he nudged his mount on down the slope.

The Flying T ranchhouse was nestled snugly in among a heavy stand of cottonwoods. Behind the trees a darker line of heavy timber rose along the sharp, vaulting flanks of the lush tableland. Still further beyond, the wooded slopes of the low hills gave way to great, thrusting patches of rockface as the foothills became mountains whose peaks, still snow-clad this far into spring, were sometimes lost in wreaths of clouds drifting in from the west.

As Zach rode into the compound, he noted that the

carpenters had finished their work. New window frames were clearly in evidence, their unpainted wood bright and clean against the log house's weathered exterior. The building, sprawled in an L among the trees, was the kind of working place a man would build without the suggestions of a woman to guide him. The bunkhouse and cookshack made up the biggest part of the building. The main house was only the base of the L, and it was this part that contained the ranch office. The barns were big, the corrals solid now that they had been repaired.

Zach rode over to the small corral, dismounted, chucked his hat back and leaned on the top rail and looked over. Manny Garcia, the running iron in his right hand, was just pulling back from the smoking hip of an unhappy cow. As Pierre LeBeau released the animal and hazed it from the corral, Thompson let in another one. The three men were working without pause.

Garcia straightened and, smiling, walked over to Zach. "Hell, boss," he said. "We all figured you'd stay hid in Canyon City 'til we got this here job done."

"That was the idea," said Zach, grinning back at the man. "Only I figured you'd be all done by this time."

The three of them laughed shortly at this.

"What do you want me to do, Manny?"

"It ain't fittin' for me to tell the boss what to do."

"Let me put it this way. You fellers look like you've got things movin' right along here. Is there anything else needs doing right now?"

Garcia sobered and nodded. "You could chase them cows we already got branded into that south flat, separate them from the rest of the herd. That would help some, Zach."

Zach nodded, turned to his horse, and mounted up. "Where's Bill and the rest of the men? Stringing wire?"

"That's what they're doin', all right."

Zach nodded, pleased. Things were shaping up better than he had figured they would, so far. Pretty soon, he knew, a very surprised Dudley Stuart would find he no longer owned half the valley, not even a third of it.

Zach had been hard at work for close to two hours when he heard the welcome jangle of the cook's triangle. He hazed the gather he had cut out through a small creek, saw them heading for the bunch already branded knee-deep in lush bottomland grass, then pulled his mount around and headed for the ranchhouse, pleased that Bill Handler had not left it to him to hire a cook.

Dismounting in front of the cookshack, Zach loosened the cinch on his horse and tramped inside. Thompson, LeBeau, and Garcia were already seated, mugs of steaming coffee in their hands. The cook was standing by the entrance to the kitchen.

He was a tall fellow with thinning, sandy hair, a mournful cast to his mouth, and watery blue eyes. A pale stubble covered his face, but it was scrubbed almost pink and a quick glance at the man's hands showed Zach that they, too, were immaculate. He had told Bill Handler that if there was one thing he could not abide, it was a cook that was not clean. Bill Handler had remembered.

"Howdy," Zach said, nodding to the cook. "I'm Zach Stuart."

"Name's Pete," said the cook, not offering anything further.

"Pleased to meet you, Pete. Welcome aboard the Flying T."

The old man nodded sourly. It was obvious he was not going to let the boss soft-soap him. He preferred to let his food do his talking.

Zach slacked his long frame down across from his three men. A pile of hot biscuits was steaming on a plate in front of him, a great slab of butter beside them on a smaller plate. A huge platter in the middle of the table contained four man-size steaks. Alongside that a bowl contained a generous helping of fried potatoes. For dessert, Zach noticed, there was a huge pork pie still steaming in its deep pie dish to one side. Zach's empty stomach was already acting up at sight of this simple but generous fare spread before them.

The cook moved discreetly out of sight as they set to work on the meal. The pork pie had completely disappeared and the cook was approaching with a fresh pot of coffee when Zach heard the drumming of a horse's hooves. Whoever it was, the rider was coming—and coming hard—from the south.

Zach glanced quickly at the others. At once the three of them bolted from the cookshack. Zach recognized the rider. It was his foreman, Bill Handler. Galloping flat out to the cookshack, the tall, red-haired foreman flung himself from his horse before it had come to a complete stop.

"Damn glad you're here, Zach!" he cried. "We got trouble!"

"You shouldn't be surprised at that, Bill."

The man grinned quickly, then sobered. "Hell, I ain't surprised. But we better get a move on. Slash D riders have surrounded all of our men, caught them stringing wire, they did. The Slash D riders are talking some about stringing the men up by that same wire."

Zach turned to the others. "Mount up."

The cook appeared in the cookshack doorway. "I'm going too," he said.

"Hell," said Zach, "I don't want to risk losing a cook like you. If you come, you stay well back."

The cook grinned, the mournful cast to his face vanishing instantly. "You mean like insurance."

"That's what I mean, Cookie," Zach said, moving to his horse and tightening the cinch.

While the rest hurried to saddle up, Bill mounted beside Zach and, as they rode out, told Zach what had happened. He had left the work party to scout the terrain ahead. On his way back to his crew, he had come across sign that indicated a large party of horsemen in the vicinity. He'd followed the sign and, sure enough, found that it led to his work party. Dismounting and traveling a small distance on foot, he had crested a knoll, peered down through the grass, and counted eight Slash D riders rousting his men.

"Was Dudley one of them?" Zach asked, absently fingering the bullwhip coiled about his saddle horn.

"Don't think so—no one that age, anyway," Bill replied. "But I saw one feller I didn't much like. A small one, pale in the face. Had a wild, pinched look about him."

"That'd be Kid Bunning, Nate Claw's *segundo*. We better slap leather."

Zach looked back. Thompson, Garcia, and LeBeau—the cook well behind—were only now trotting from the compound. When they saw Zach turn about in his saddle, the four riders promptly lifted their horses to a lope. Zach glanced swiftly back at Bill.

"Lead the way," he said.

After almost an hour's hard ride, they left their horses in among some rocks and, with Bill leading, angled down a short slope; they crossed a stream, cut across a lush meadow where the grass was already knee high, then up to the crest of a steep knoll. By the time they peered over it, they were on their bellies, each one with his rifle out and ready. The cook, panting slightly, droppped to the ground beside Zach. He was lugging an old Walker Colt and an almost equally ancient Henry repeater.

"I told you to stay back," said Zach softly.

"You didn't say how far back," growled the man, his long, mournful face set grimly. "Besides," he went on, without changing expression, "this is the first real excitement I've had since a buffalo tore up my chuck wagon in Dakota." He frowned at Zach. "And you ain't gonna make me miss it."

"Wouldn't think of arguin' with the cook," said Zach with a smile.

Looking back down the slope, he saw that the situation was unfriendly enough, but still in a building stage. Mounted Slash D riders with drawn guns were directing Zach's men to complete the demolition of the wagon with sledge hammers. The wagon was pretty far gone by this time, and most of Zach's men were now busy uprooting posts and snipping wires.

Looking back along the wire that had been strung, Zach saw that most of it was hanging loosely. It had been cut in so many places, it would be impossible to repair. All new wire would have to be strung. New posts would have to be sunk as well.

Zach told Thompson and Garcia to work their way to the north, keep low in the grass and not show themselves, but work in as close to the action as possible. He told Pierre to go south and do the same thing. They were to stay out of it unless it looked as if Zach and Bill were in real trouble. It was Zach's intention to ride down with Bill and explain peaceably why Flying T was now fencing this range.

The cook grumbled something.

Zach looked at him. "What's wrong, Cookie?"

"You just gonna ride down there—leave yourself open to them buzzards?"

"Not really, Pete. Can you work that Henry?"

"This little sweetheart can goose a prairie chicken at fifty yards."

"Fine. You stay right here and keep your rifle at the ready." Zach looked around him at the others. "I'm going to give you fellers about ten minutes to get into position. Bill and I are relying on you to back our play."

The three men nodded grimly.

"Okay, then. Move out."

As the men left ridge and moved off through the tall grass, Zach and Bill went back for their horses.

A Flying T hand, who had just finished bringing his sledge hammer down through a wheel spoke, looked up to mop his brow and spotted Zach and Bill cresting the ridge. Zach saw the look on the fellow's face. The pure relief was almost comical. A moment later they were spotted by the Slash D riders.

Zach found himself once again measuring Nate Claw and the Kid. Dudley had certainly picked himself a couple of hard cases to run his spread for him. They were killers, both of them. Their tight faces creased into unpleasant smiles as they saw Zach and Bill riding into their midst.

At a sharp command from Nate Claw, the Slash D riders swung their mounts around to face Zach and Bill. Then they drifted into a wide semicircle into which Zach and Bill rode. Sunlight glinted menacingly off their sidearms as they lifted the bores.

Nate Claw spoke first. "Hold up right there, Stuart."

Zach pulled his horse slowly to a stop, Bill reining in beside him. "You're on Flying T land, Nate. And you're destroying Flying T property. I'll expect proper compensation from the owner of the Slash D." Zach smiled. "Looks like you're costing him money."

"You know that's a damn lie," Nate spat. "This is Slash D range—always has been and always will be."

"Always has been, maybe. But no more, Nate. I own it now. It's part of the Flying T."

"Flying T?"

"Never heard of it, eh?"

"Sure, I heard of it. That's Jane Durrell's property. You working it for her? You taking orders from a whore?"

"I bought the ranch from Jane," Zach said evenly, "and some additional quarter sections as well. Been doing so for some time, I might add. That's why the land you are on is no longer Slash D's. I have bought this land, Nate."

Nate glanced for a moment at the Kid. He understood Zach's words, all right. It was their significance he found difficult to grasp. How could Zach own this land? How could Dudley Stuart have allowed such a thing? Zach could see the incredulity on Nate's face and, along with it, a stubborn refusal to accept the truth of Zach's words.

"Maybe you think you bought this land," Nate said. "But we've got the drop on you and your men, and as far as I can see, you're on Slash D land; tresspassin', I calls it. Unbuckle your gunbelt, Stuart. You, too, mister," he said, addressing Bill.

"Slowlike," reminded the Kid.

As Zach's gunbelt struck the ground, Zach said, "You'd better be reasonable, Nate. You're on Flying T land. The law won't see this any other way."

"Hell," chuckled Nate. "The Slash D *is* the law in these parts."

"Look," began Zach, still trying to talk sense, "you've already cut our wire and destroyed our wagon. If you hurt any of us you'll cause a stink even Dudley Stuart won't be able to hush up."

"Say, there," Nate said, "what do you take us for—animals? We're just going to take you and your *segundo* back to the Slash D to talk to your old man. We figure you should explain all that bullshit about buying this land to him, personal."

The Kid smiled. Zach heard a few of the Slash D riders chuckling softly among themselves. They understood—as did Zach—what Nate really intended. Since the Belle Fourche, these two had a score to settle with Zach. He and Bill had about as much chance of surviving that long ride to the Slash D as a wax cat in hell.

"Just one thing," Zach said, as if he had accepted the necessity of going with them back to the Slash D. "Let my men go. You've deviled them enough."

"Why, sure," Nate said. He turned in his saddle and nodded to his men.

The six Slash D riders lowered their guns and watched as Zach's men hurried on foot past the riders and started up the slope. Zach called out to one of them to go back for the horse team. Then he sat his horse calmly alongside Bill and watched as the men scrambled up the knoll. When the team of horses, their traces dragging behind them, dropped beyond the crest, Zach looked back at Nate.

"Let's go, then," he said.

Nate's men had been lulled by all this. Three had already holstered their weapons. They urged their riders to the rear of Zach and Bill, while Nate and the Kid started to turn their mounts to ride ahead of them. The instant Nate's eyes left Zach's, Zach snatched up his bullwhip and, with an expertness born of years of practice, sent its lash whistling through the air, its rawhide tip coiling about Nate's neck with a stinging crack.

Even as the crack sounded, Zach was spurring his horse forward and to the right. As Nate reached up to grab the rawhide that had encircled his throat, Zach, riding at full gallop, yanked viciously and dragged the Slash D foreman from his saddle. The man struck the ground on his right shoulder and began frantically trying to free himself from the whip's embrace as he rolled over in the high grass, still being dragged along by Zach.

Pulling up, Zach flicked the lash expertly, releasing it from around the man's neck, snapped it back, and then sent it whistling out again. This time the lash encircled the Kid's wrist. With a yelp of pain he dropped his six-gun. At that moment the crack of a Henry sounded from the knoll behind Zach. Glancing swiftly back over his shoulder, Zach saw one of the Slash D riders peeling from his horse.

The crack of other rifles sounded, coming from the grass on both sides of them. A Slash D rider lost his hat. Another saw his gun go flying from a bloody hand. Thompson, Garcia, and LeBeau were on their feet by this time, striding forward through the tall grass, their rifles at the ready. The rest of the Slash D riders dropped their weapons and flung their hands skyward.

Swinging back to the Kid, Zach saw him tugging at the lash still coiled about his narrow wrist. Zach yanked, forcing the Kid to leap headlong from his saddle, landing in the heavy grass beside Nate. Dismounting, Zach advanced on the two, coiling his whip as he went. Furious, the two men scrambled to their feet.

"Drop your gunbelt, Nate," Zach said.

Nate did. Zach turned to the other riders. "Get off your horses," he told them.

As the men dismounted, Bill Handler went over to inspect the Slash D rider Cookie's shot had caught in the shoulder. The man was sitting up, holding his wound. Examining it quickly, Bill called back, "It's just a flesh wound, Zach. He'll live."

The rider who had lost his gun was on his feet, holding his shattered hand and cursing softly to himself. Bill examined the hand, then returned to Zach. "He'll likely lose a finger," he told him.

"Okay. Give that fellow with the shoulder wound a horse," Zach told Bill.

Bill nodded.

Zach raised his voice so that all could hear him. "The rest of you men can walk back to the Slash D."

"Walk!" Nate cried, furious.

"That's right. Walk. All the way. We'll keep your horseflesh at my ranch. Dudley can send someone over for them later—with the hundred dollars I'll need to get a new wagon and more wire."

Nate Claw turned away, fuming. Zach knew why he was so furious. There were only two things that truly terrified a cowboy—a decent woman and being left afoot. As soon as Bill had helped the Slash D rider with the shoulder wound back up onto his horse, Zach stepped back.

"All right, Slash D!" he called. "Move out! Now!"

Trudging off with the Kid, Nate did not bother to reply or look back. But Zach wasn't worried. He knew his message would get through. The Flying T had just declared war on the Slash D. What remained now was for Zach to get the rest of the ranchers in this valley together.

And the sooner he did that, the better.

Six

DUDLEY SWORE. WHAT SILAS had just told him with a smirk on his grizzled face was true. Nate and the Kid, on foot, were approaching the ranch at the head of five men, also on foot, strung out in a long, disorderly line that reached almost to the horizon. The only man on a horse was a little bit ahead of them, and he looked ready at any moment to topple from his saddle.

Chuckling, Silas said, “You want I should send out a wagon for them poor miserable bastards?”

Dudley shook his head emphatically. “No! Let them walk. And go get rest of the men in the bunkhouse. I want them to watch this bunch straggle in. Might serve as a useful lesson.”

It was Silas who caught the wounded Johnny Winner as he slipped, barcly conscious, from his saddle. Dudley was back on the porch, watching it all grimly. Nate and the Kid, looking as woebegone and sullen as whipped curs, trudged wearily across the compound toward him. When both men pulled up in front of the porch, Dudley studied them for a moment, then smiled coldly and told them to get into his office.

Oncc he was settled in his chair, the two men still on their feet, facing him across the desk, he asked them what the hell they were doing afoot.

“We tangled with Zach Stuart,” Nate said.

"He bushwhacked us," said the Kid.

"Zach? I thought he had left these parts."

"He's back. We come onto a crew of his putting up fencing across North Flats."

"You say Zach's crew?"

Nate nodded, his eyes narrowing as he watched Dudley's reaction. "He owns the Flying T. And he told me to tell you that he owns that flat, too. That's why he was fencing it."

"The Flying T? That spread belongs to Jane Durrell."

"It did," said the Kid venomously. "Seems like that makes pretty good sense to me—after seeing them two at the funeral."

Nate cleared his throat nervously. "Seems like he thinks he owns a lot of land, not just that flat. He talked pretty confident."

Dudley's mind was racing. At the graveside, Zach had said he was going to take all this from him. His words then had seemed like the preposterous threats of a grieving, angry son. Now, he saw at once, they were more than that. Much more.

"What about our horses?" Dudley asked wearily.

"Zach told us you could send someone after them—with a hundred dollars to pay for the damage we done to his wagon and his fences."

"You want to explain that?" Dudley snapped angrily.

"We made the Flying T's crew wreck the wagon they were using to haul the barbed wire," explained the Kid. As he spoke, he glanced almost pleadingly at one of the chairs against the wall. Dudly ignored his evident discomfort.

"And we cut most of the wire they strung," Nate said.

Dudley was seething internally at the apparent ease with which this son of his was able to turn the tables on these two sore-footed hard cases standing before him. But he spoke to the men in as calm a fashion as he could manage under the circumstances. "All right, then. I'll send Silas with the money for the horses. You two get cleaned up and tell Cookie to feed you. First thing in the morning, the three of us are going in to Canyon City."

The Kid's eyes narrowed, his sallow face seeming to sharpen. "We goin' to visit that whore in the Belle Fourche, Mr. Stuart?"

"First," said Dudley, "we'll visit the land office and find out just what the hell Zach was talking about. Then maybe we'll visit the Belle Fourche." He paused. "Now, do you two think maybe you can handle that?"

The two did not reply. The stinging sarcasm in Dudley's tone left them no defense. They turned and stomped from Dudley's office, seething. Dudley was pleased. This would prime them well for what he had in mind the next day.

He reached into a drawer for his whiskey bottle and poured himself a drink. He was thinking of Jane Durrell. She, along with Miss Helen, had conspired with his son against him. All these years she had served him and his men drinks without once letting on that Dudley had a son. At times, when the mood came upon him and not even Felicia could quell the fires of hell that consumed him, he had gone to her in his naked need and she had provided him with a girl young enough and tireless enough to satisfy his demands.

In short, Jane Durrell had presented herself to him as a friend—a casual friend, to be sure. But a friend, nevertheless. It seemed to Dudley that her perfidy stank to high heaven.

He would tend to her.

Dudley left the land office early that next afternoon with a scowl on his face. It was worse than he could have imagined. And Jane Durrell's involvement was even more flagrant than he had imagined. He had left the clerk a mass of quivering jelly by the time he got through questioning him and going over the deeds.

But it was not the clerk's fault. It was his own fault. He should have purchased that land long ago. The days of the open range were fast disappearing. He had seen it coming as had most other big ranchers. The trouble was he had not seen any trouble coming from the ranchers in this valley. With the exception of Snyder and that toothless Association of theirs, the smaller ranchers had kept their tails between their legs and done their best to stay out of his way.

But now Zach had boxed him in—legally.

Nate and the Kid were waiting for him outside the land office. Slouched against the hitch rail, they straightened as he approached. "Let's get a drink, boys," Dudley told them.

The Kid smiled. The look of it gave Dudley a momentary shudder. As the three of them moved along the sidewalk to the Belle Fourche, Dudley hung back slightly, allowing Nate and the Kid to enter ahead of him. When he finally pushed his way through the batwings, he saw them bellying up to the bar.

It was early, a little after the noon hour. The place was quiet. Only one poker game was in progress. Two drummers at the far end of the bar were nursing their whiskeys. As Dudley sat carefully in a chair behind a table along the far wall, he watched Nate rap sharply on the gleaming mahogany bar with the barrel of his six-gun. The barkeep, an irritated frown on his face, hastened down the bar to tend to Nate.

Dudley heard the barkeep—his name was Stan—tell Nate to put away his gun or he wouldn't serve him. Nate laughed and fired a bullet into the mirror behind the bar, spider-webbing it. The round missed the bartender by what must have been at best a fraction of an inch. The barkeep looked as if he wanted to piss and sit down at the same time. The Kid reached across the top of the bar, grabbed the man around his shirt collar, pulled his shoulders down onto the bar, took out his six-gun and rested the barrel on the man's cheek just under his left eye.

"Hey, now, listen!" the fellow bleated. "What the hell you two guys up to?"

"Get that whore what runs this place," Nate told him. "Now!"

The town constable entered at just that moment. The single shot must have drawn him. Hope flooded the barkeep's face as he spied Wally standing uncertainly in front of the still swinging batwings.

"Wally!" Dudley barked. "Get over here!"

Wally, a puzzled look on his jowly face, hurried over to Dudley's table. "Sure, Dudley. What is it? What's going on?"

"Nothing you need concern yourself with, Wally. Go back to your office and keep Pike and any of your deputies out of this, too. That clear?"

The constable glanced unhappily over at the bar, then back to Dudley. "Sure thing, Dudley. You know you can count on me."

Wally turned and quickly disappeared out the saloon door. Dudley looked back at his two men and nodded briskly for them to get on with it. By this time, the card players in the back of the place had vanished out the rear door and the two drummers were cat-footing it swiftly from the place.

The Kid let go of the barkeep. The fellow almost collapsed out of sight behind the bar before he recovered and hurried down its length. Smiling, Dudley watched him knock swiftly on the door to Jane Durrell's office. A sleepy, unkempt Jane Durrell pulled the door open. This early, she was not fully dressed and was wearing a long pink housecoat with a large, fluffy collar. Holding it about her, she frowned irritably at the barkeep and asked him why he had awakened her.

The barkeep pointed down the bar at Nate and the Kid. She blinked in the dim light in an effort to take in what the two men wanted. Then she evidently caught sight of the revolvers in their hands, and straightened up in alarm. The Kid laughed. It was a low, menacing chuckle that almost raised the hair on the back of Dudley's neck. Dudley leaned back in his chair, savoring the look of quiet, resigned despair on the fat slut's face.

It was obvious to her what Nate and the Kid were about.

"All they want," said Dudley quietly to her, his voice carrying easily across the now deserted saloon, "is some early entertainment."

"My girls," Jane said, "are still sleeping. I always let them sleep until three. Tell your boys to come back then." It was a brave try, Dudley conceded. But the tremble in her voice betrayed her.

"Now you know they don't want students," Dudley said. "They want the teacher. Isn't that right, boys?"

Nate and the Kid nodded. They holstered their guns and started for the woman. The barkeep turned about then and placed himself in front of Jane. He was scared clean through to the soles of his boots, but he was game.

"Get out of the way, Stan," Dudley told the barkeep. "Or my boys will kill you. If they don't, I will."

As he spoke, Dudley removed his Colt from its holster, laid it down on the top of the table, and deliberately cocked it. Stan moistened dry lips and looked desperately around. He was hoping for a miracle. Only there wasn't going to be one.

"Take him, boys," said Dudley.

Nate reached Stan first and pistol-whipped him viciously about the face until the man pitched forward onto the sawdust, his broken face dribbling blood. Jane held herself erect, her hands at her sides, her robe falling open.

"All right, boys," she said icily. "School's in session."

She turned and led the way into her office. It was the Kid, a cold smile frozen on his narrow face, who closed the door behind them. Dudley got up and walked around behind the bar and poured himself a drink. He brought the glass and the bottle back to his table. No sound came from beyond the closed door.

He was on his second glass when a patron poked his head carefully in through the batwings. There had been the sound of a crowd gathering outside the saloon, but Dudley had simply ignored it. Amused, Dudley watched the fellow's eyes looking about the apparently deserted saloon. The first thing the fellow saw was the unconscious barkeep lying in a pool of his own blood. Then he saw Dudley watching him.

Dudley lifted the cocked revolver and leveled it at the fellow. "Get out of here," he said.

The man vanished.

Dudley was pouring his third glass when he heard a muffled cry from Jane's office. He smiled. It was about time they got to her. A moment later he heard something heavy strike the wall alongside the door, followed by another cry, louder this time.

Dudley took his time finishing his third drink, picked up his Colt, and walked over to the door, past the still unconscious barkeep. He could hear Jane crying softly now. He opened the door and walked in. The whore was crumpled on the floor alongside the door, not a stitch left on her. Her face and shoulders were a mass of purplish welts. As she wept, he saw she had lost two teeth. One nostril was pouring blood.

"What happened?" Dudley asked mildly.

"The stinking bitch bit me," Nate replied.

The Kid stood there, grinning. Indicating Nate with a quick nod, he said, "Nate almost lost his manhood."

Neither man had his pants on. Their faces were flushed, their hair damp. As they stood looking down at Jane Durrell's ample nakedness, their breathing came in large, gasping bursts. They had been having one helluva time, Dudley realized.

"Is she a good teacher, boys?"

"I've had better," said Nate, grinning weakly.

"That's not kind, Nate."

"No," said the Kid, "but it's true."

"Outside," Dudley told them.

The two men hastily pulled on their britches, found their hats, and hurried out past Dudley. Dudley looked down at the naked woman. She was still weeping softly.

"Get out of this town, Jane," he told her. "This is only a taste of what I'll do to you—and to your girls—if you stay. I'll send my whole crew in here if you don't believe me. Sell out and get out. So I'll know you aim to do what I'm telling you, close up the Belle Fourche now. I'll expect you on a train by the weekend." He smiled. "And I am sure that the better element in Canyon City will applaud my action in ridding this place of your kind."

Jane pulled herself to her feet, one hand clasping what was left of her robe and holding it against her. Her face had begun to swell noticeably. "I don't care," she whispered fiercely. "It's all right what happens to me—just so long as you get what's coming to you. And you will! Zach will see to that!"

For a moment Dudley had an urge to respond. But it would be demeaning for him to stand there and argue with a naked whore. He stepped back out of the room and pulled the door shut behind him.

The barkeep was stirring groggily, his big hands moving sluggishly through the heavy layer of sawdust on the floor. He blinked up at Dudley uncomprehendingly, his face a mass of sawdust and gore.

"Don't get up yet, Stan," Dudley advised, as he stepped around the man. "Stay right where you are if you value your life."

Nate and the Kid were waiting for him in front of the bar. He nodded to them. They took our their six-guns and began peppering the mirror, the shelves, and everything they could use as a target. The detonations thundered in the place with such force that Dudley found it difficult to keep from wincing. When the two finished shooting up the bar, they directed their attention to the chandeliers. As soon as the crystal had been reduced to splintered shards, they finished off by blasting holes in the mural over the bar and then through any other pictures that caught their fancy.

Dudley caught sight of two terrified girls peering from around the staircase leading to their rooms upstairs.

"Get out of here, girls," Dudley told them. "This here stinkhole is out of business. Go on back upstairs and pack!"

The girls ducked out of sight; Dudley heard their feet on the stairs. Then he turned and nodded to Nate and the Kid. The three men strode from the saloon. A large crowd had gathered by this time, and as the three of them appeared, those men standing in the front ranks backed up hastily.

"Put up your guns," Dudley told his two men.

As they did so, Dudley looked around the crowd. It was predominantly male, mostly townsmen and local shopkeepers, with a sprinkling of bonnetted women and a few youngsters.

"The excitement's over, folks," Dudley announced. "The Belle Fourche is now out of business."

"What happened in there, Dudley?" someone at the rear of the crowd yelled.

"Why, nothing, really. Just a little misunderstanding. Seems that Jane Durrell backed the wrong hombre—and lost." He smiled, tugged down his hat, and started through the crowd on the way to his horse. "Looks like you men will just have to take your trade elsewhere."

There was a puzzled murmur at that, but no one dared step forward to question Dudley, and not a voice was raised to stop him as he rode out of town with Nate Claw and Kid Bunning a few moments later.

Seven

THAT SAME DAY, ON toward evening, Zach and a somewhat subdued group of ranchers met at Dave Snyder's Diamond Cross. Each one of the ranchers had already heard what Dudley Stuart and his two lieutenants had done to Jane Durrell and her barkeep. As a warning to his enemies, and these ranchers in particular, it could not have been more effective.

Zach had arrived earlier and had been introduced to the other ranchers by Snyder. The man had done this without much grace. Snyder was evidently still smarting from the way Zach had dealt with him earlier in the Belle Fourche. Now Zach was sitting in the small parlor while the others sat at a long table in the kitchen and discussed in low, urgent tones just how they were going to handle this proposal of Zach's that they combine forces.

As Zach waited, trying not to overhear their debate, he could still see in his mind's eye the bruised body of Jane Durrell and the shattered face of her barkeep. The land office clerk had mustered what remained of his courage after Dudley's visit and had loaded Jane and the barkeep into his carriage and dropped them off at the Flying T before continuing on out of the valley. Cookie was not sure he knew what to do about Stan's left eye, and Zach had sent into Canyon City for a doctor.

Earlier that same day, when Dudley's wrangler, a tired old man, arrived with a more than generous payment for

Zach's ruined wagon and a request for Slash D's horses, Zach had been caught off guard. He had found it difficult to understand Dudley's easy capitulation—until the old wrangler, as he rode out with the Slash D stock, leaned around in his saddle and told him not to let this fool him none, that Dudley was a man who hated better than he did anything else.

The significance of that old man's remark had soon enough become apparent when Zach saw Jane and the barkeep. If there was a Lucifer in residence on this planet, his name was Dudley Stuart; and this valley, it seemed, was his own hellish playground.

A chair scraped in the kitchen. Dave Snyder appeared in the kitchen doorway. "Come on in, Zach," he said. "I guess we're ready for you now."

They had left a chair for him at one end of the table in front of the stove. A few sticks of wood were burning in the pot belly in an effort to banish the damp spring chill. The men were passing two coffee pots down the long table. Snyder sat himself down at the far end of the table and spoke quietly for a moment with the Stirrup owner, Ken Sullivan.

Sullivan was a man in his late forties, tough-looking, heavy-browed, with a luxuriant shock of dark hair. He had a silver flask on the table in front of him and was lacing his coffee liberally as he listened to Snyder. Sullivan's foreman, Tobe Winston, a small, red-faced, scrawny-necked old timer, sat beside Sullivan, talking softly to the owner sitting across from him.

This was Sven Torgeson, the owner of the Running H. Torgeson was a blue-eyed giant of a man with a deceptively soft voice who spoke excellent English except for occasional lapses into his native Swedish. He was in his early fifties; his full head of hair was almost completely white. His daughter had come along. Her name was Sue, and she was standing beside the stove, talking softly to Dave Snyder's wife. Sue had brought along fresh doughnuts, which were sitting on the counter, waiting for the close of the meeting when they would be passed around.

Sue was pretty. Zach had little difficulty in imagining what her flaxen hair would look like with its fullness released from the tight bun into which it had been wound. Such thoughts, however, were beyond the pale at this moment. When Sue Torgeson had been introduced to him by her father, her eyes had flicked over him quite coldly, and he knew at once that she saw in him only a dangerous echo of Dudley Stuart.

Snyder looked away from Ken Sullivan and rapped a spoon against the side of his coffee mug.

"I guess it's time for us to hear what Zach has to say," Snyder announced stiffly. "Officially, this is just one more meeting of the Small Ranchers Association." He glanced unhappily at two empty chairs. "But it looks like the Bar B and the Singletree will not be represented this evening." Snyder looked coldly down the table at Zach. "Okay, Zach. You got the floor."

"Thanks, Dave," Zach said. "Wish we could wait a little longer for the others, but I guess we've waited long enough." He paused a moment, looked down at his hands clenched before him on the table, then back up at the faces turned to him. "And I suppose that's what I've come to tell you. You've all waited long enough—and so have I. Now the time has come for us to stand up to Dudley, to refuse to let him push us around. If we stick together, work together, and don't let him take us on one at a time, we can stop him. What I'm saying is from now on, if he leans on one, he leans on all of us. That will let him know he no longer owns this valley. As a matter of fact, you know, his actual holdings are small and scattered. He really *doesn't* own this valley any more."

"No," growled Sullivan, cocking one bushy eyebrow, "you do."

"Let's just say I own what it takes to reduce the Slash D to its legal boundaries. I've left Dudley's spread two pretty fair sources of water, Indian Springs and a stretch bordering the Little Whiskey. It won't be enough to water the size of the herds he's running now, but it will simply have to do."

"And you know damn well," said Sullivan, his heavy voice carrying powerfully in the crowded room, "that it won't do—not for that man. You've got the devil himself by the tail, me bucko, and you know it."

"You make it sound so simple," spoke up Sven Torgeson. "Just stick together. And you say if we do, Dudley Stuart will accept what you have done, yah?"

"He has to. What I have done is perfectly legal. He'll be going against the law if he tries to graze on any land that is not his—or if he trespasses on my land to get to water."

"Like my spring at Twin Forks," said Snyder.

"Exactly," agreed Zach. "And that Sweetwater Range of yours I understand he has been using."

"Don't forget my northern pastures," put in Sullivan. "He's already hazing some of his stock up in there to take advantage of the spring growth."

"There's just one thing," said Torgeson softly.

"What's that?" asked Zach.

"Dudley Stuart *is* the law in this valley. The town marshal is in his back pocket. And he owns that Sheriff Pike, lock, stock, and barrel."

"And most every townsman with power in Canyon City," agreed Sullivan. "They are all his poker pals."

"Which means," said Sullivan's foreman, his voice a gentle rasp, as he turned to address Zach for the first time, "that, legal or not, we don't have much recourse if Dudley goes into one of his fits."

"Like he did today in Canyon City," Torgeson reminded them all ominously.

Zach waited before responding. He didn't want to minimize the threat Dudley posed to each one of them, but he could not allow their fear of the man to carry the day. "We have recourse," Zach said quietly. "If Sheriff

Pike won't keep Dudley in line, we can send to the capital, to the Attorney General's office, and request a federal U.S deputy marshal be sent in here."

"That will take time," said Sullivan. "And Dudley Stuart has powerful friends in the State House, all of them cattle men from the old days when open range was a kind of religion. We've tried to get a rope on that man for years. What makes you think it's going to be so easy this time, Zach?"

"It isn't," replied Zach. "I know that. But this time you've got my outfit on your side. I've boxed Dudley in all nice and proper. Whatever he does now will put him outside the law—completely. And once he steps over that line, we'll have him."

"Give him enough rope, you mean," said Sullivan.

"Yes."

"What's your interest in all this, Zach?" Torgeson asked quietly. "Why are you so anxious to save our bacon?"

Zach glanced down the table at the grim faces waiting for his response. He shrugged. "I think you know why I'm here and what my interest in stopping Dudley Stuart is," he replied softly. "I am just suggesting that we might work together—to our mutual advantage."

Sullivan straightened in his seat and rested the palms of his hands facedown on the table. "All right," he said, his voice resonant with decision. "As long as Zach is talking straight with us, I say take advantage of the situation. Dudley is our cat to bell, looks like. And this young bucko here is just the one for the job."

Torgeson cleared his throat. Zach turned to the man. "I can only say," Torgeson began carefully, almost regretfully, "that I do not like cornering a man like Dudley Stuart. He is not a rational man." Torgeson looked closely at Zach. "And it seems to me that we have a rather unpleasant situation—an irrational man and a son who hates him enough to want to destroy him." The man shook his head sadly. "It is ugly. That is the only word I can find to describe how I feel." He smiled wanly at Zach. "No hard feelings, Zach."

Torgeson's words left everyone at the table thoughtful. Zach waited a decent interval, then he glanced at Snyder.

"I'm for it," said Snyder, "but I think first we should contact our other members before we come to any binding decision on the matter."

"Hell," said Sullivan softly. "The others have already voted. With their feet. They knew about this meeting. They'd be happy if Dudley Stuart caught a cold and dropped dead, but they ain't going to do anything to see to it that he catches a cold. I say we decide right now to throw in with Zach."

"I'll stick with Sully," said Sven Torgeson, shrugging his shoulders. "Like he says, maybe Zach is the fellow to bell the cat. We sure ain't been doing such a fine job ourselves."

Snyder sighed, looked just once more around the table for any more comment, then glanced at Zach. "That's it, then," he said. "But I think you should go talk to the other ranchers yourself, Zach."

Zach nodded. "I'll do that."

Snyder glanced back at his wife. "Mary, those doughnuts Sue brought sure look good."

As Snyder's wife passed around the platter of doughnuts, Zach found it easy to see why her husband had such a sour disposition. There seemed no softness about the woman, no comfort in her long face or bleak eyes. As she paused beside Zach with the platter, her mouth became a straight, disapproving line, her glance withering. Like her husband, it seemed, she was not entirely on his side.

The conversation among the other ranchers turned to more general topics, and as soon as Zach could decently do so, he got to his feet, shook hands all around, and excused himself. He explained how anxious he was to get back to his ranch to see to Jane. At mention of Jane, Mary Snyder's face went pale with disapproval.

Sue was standing at the door with his hat. She handed it to him, her smile icy. In a soft but urgent voice, she said, "Why don't you go back to wherever you came from, Zach Stuart? Leave your father be—and let us handle him in our own way. We do not want to become part of your vendetta."

Zach took his hat from her and smiled. "I understand how you feel, Miss Torgeson. I would feel the same way if I were in your shoes. By the way, those doughnuts *were* delicious."

He nodded curtly to her and left.

Jane was sitting up in his bed. She looked surprisingly chipper, despite her bruised forehead and cheeks and the lopsided cast to her face. The doctor had come and gone, taking Stan back with him to Canyon City.

Jane managed a smile. "How did it go, Zach?"

"About as I expected. How do you feel?"

"Better than I look, I'm sure."

"How's Stan?"

"He might lose his eye, Zach. The doctor took Stan back with him so he could keep a closer tab on him."

Zach nodded. "Cookie told me."

"I want to get up tomorrow and go back into Canyon City, Zach. I want to reopen the Belle Fourche. Only this time I'm keeping a loaded shotgun handy."

Zach frowned. "Easy now. You sure that's what you really want? Maybe that land office clerk had the right idea—clear out. When this mess is over, I'll write you and you can come back."

"I'm staying. I want to be here when you nail that skunk's hide to the wall."

Zach looked at Jane for a long moment. This was the same woman who used to play with him on sunny meadows and read to him at bedtime so many years ago that to remember was like trying to recall a forgotten dream. Jane had been a young girl then and full of laughter—one of Miss Helen's most popular attractions. Now he and Jane were together again; only this time he was a grown man and Jane was an oversized woman, no longer pretty, filled not with the soft warmth he remembered but with a corrosive hatred she had honed to a cutting edge over the years. Her letters to Zach about Dudley had dripped venom. It was as if, having been left in Canyon City with no one to love, she had fed on her hatred of Zach's father instead.

Zach sat carefully down on the side of the bed. Jane reached out and took one of his hands in hers and squeezed it. Zach smiled down at the battered visage sunken into the pillow.

"What's the matter, Zach?" she asked. "You ain't getting cold feet, are you?"

"No, I don't think so."

"You sure looked mighty thoughtful for a moment there. Didn't you think I meant it when I said I want to go back to the Belle Fourche?"

"I know you meant it. It's just that I wouldn't want anything else to happen to you."

"I told you. I'll keep a shotgun handy."

"That may not be enough."

"I don't care," Jane said, smiling with difficulty and revealing a gap where she had lost a couple of teeth. "Just so's we get Dudley."

Zach found himself remembering Sue Torgeson's words: *Leave your father be—and let us handle him in our own way. We do not want to become part of your vendetta.*

Vendetta. Yes, that was what it was. And Sue's father was right. It *was* ugly.

Gently, Zach disengaged his hand from Jane's and stood up. "It's late, Jane. If you're going back into Canyon City, you're not going for a couple of days yet, and that's an order. You took care of me often enough. Now it's my turn. Hear?"

Jane smiled—and for a moment that other Jane from long ago peered up at him once again, as she had that first day in her office. "All right, Zach. I'll rest up first. I just didn't want you to think them bastards could lick me. And don't forget. The Belle Fourche is all I got."

"I understand, Jane," he said.

He blew out the lamp, then bid her goodnight and closed the door. The house was silent as he walked down the hall and out into the cool spring night. A gleaming canopy of stars hung just overhead. Zach leaned back against the log wall of the ranchhouse and built himself a cigarette.

With his arms folded, his hat tilted well back off his forehead, he let Lady Nicotine comfort him as best she could. He was aware that he should be furious at what Dudley Stuart had done that day to Jane Durrell and Stan. And he did feel outraged.

Yet who really was to blame? Zach had let it be known that he would like nothing better than a confrontation. He had declared war on his father. So the man had struck back at Zach's closest ally for openers.

Zach sighed deeply, a frown on his face. It was simply not as clear-cut as it was supposed to be. Zach knew what he should do—and what he *would* do. But poor Stan's condition and that of Jane Durrell, asleep now in his bed, gave him a sobering glimpse of what lay ahead for all of them once the battle between Zach and his father was truly joined.

Zach finished his smoke at last, flicked the glowing butt into the darkness, and went back into the ranchhouse to bed.

Eight

ALONE, DUDLEY SAT HIS horse atop the rise and looked down at the flat. The barbed wire stretched in both directions as far as he could see, like teeth sunk into his soul. It infuriated him—but in the end he was helpless. He could cut the damn stuff at one place only to find it repaired within the week. Even as he watched, Dudley saw a Flying T fence rider gallop into view.

Dudley pulled his rifle quickly from its sleeve, levered a fresh cartridge into the chamber, then sighted on the rider. He tracked the lone horseman until he was less than a couple of hundred yards away—an easy shot for Dudley—then continued to track him. Before the fence rider was out of sight, Dudley pulled his rifle down and stared gloomily after the rider. When his men had told him about the increasing network of barbed wire enclosing the Slash D, he had ordered them to cut through and ignore it. But this day he had ridden far and wide to find the gleaming network everywhere, a vicious barbed web that now completely ensnared the Slash D. Like a trussed and helpless fly, the Slash D was waiting for its lifeblood to be sucked from it.

The only way that he could see to break out of this wire trap was to destroy those men who had strung it across his range—to root them out and truss them in the same barbed impediment they were using to strangle the Slash D. *But that meant he had to destroy Zach, as well.*

As Dudley now knew, such a course was impossible for him. A part of him raged at the thought of his son's terrible insolence—but another part of him could not contemplate his boy's death. He had destroyed his wife, the boy's mother; the thought of destroying his son also was simply too fearsome to contemplate.

But that did not mean he was helpless before his son's assault. He could strip away Zach's allies, his pawns in this deadly game. Once Zach was alone—finally—on this chess board, perhaps then he would see the folly of continuing the game. Blood should not fight blood; it was in truth thicker than water.

Dudley wheeled his horse and left the ridge.

Sven Torgeson would not have arrived late back at the ranch if he had not ridden over to inspect Cedar Flats.

He and his men had just finished a week of hazing better than half of his stock down out of the foothills, and he was pleased with the amount of tallow still on his cows, very pleased indeed. The herd, especially the calves, had wintered well.

His inspection of Cedar Flats had been encouraging. The heavy spring rains had already brought forth a lush first growth. The flats, he was certain, could easily handle the rest of his herd, those he had wintered in the south flats along Milk Creek.

The lazy, pleasant drift of Sven's thoughts was broken into by the sound of distant gunfire. He pulled up abruptly. No doubt about it. Shots. A dim, popping sound, and it was coming from just over the next ridge—and that meant the Running H!

He spurred his horse, crested the ridge, and galloped down the long, sweeping meadow toward the dim cluster of his ranch buildings half a mile away. Gunfire was pouring into the compound the cottonwoods and the wooded bluffs overlooking the ranchhouse. Soon Sven was close enough to attract fire. He kept galloping full tilt on toward the barn until one slug caught the brim of his hat and tugged it back off his head. If it were not for the chin strap, he would have lost it. He swerved, galloped parallel to the barn for a few minutes, found himself again a target, and veered away back toward the ridge, cursing in Swedish, his face dark with fury.

Watching, helpless, from a low, pine-studded ridge, his outrage slowly gave way to puzzlement. The fire from the attackers was desultory. No volleys were sustained for any length of time; no attempts were made to rush the ranch buildings. After a while the firing almost ceased. Only gunfire from one of Sven's men hiding somewhere in the compound brought a response, after which the gunfire would promptly die away again.

It was not an attack. Sven felt that it in his bones. It was a diversion, a holding operation. For some reason this group of Slash D riders—he could not imagine any other outfit sending men against him—had been sent to pin down him and his riders within the Running H compound.

Why?

Instantly he knew.

He pulled his mount around, whipped out his quirt, and began punishing his mount as he galloped back to the herd they had just gathered. As he rode, he cursed himself for not having left a few men behind to guard it. Dudley's apparent acceptance these past weeks of his new situation had lulled Sven and the other ranchers into a false sense of security. Just as it was supposed to do.

The Kid stood up in his stirrups and looked over the backs of the cattle. He smiled. Dusk was falling, but he was able to see clearly the herd's impressive size. The small valley floor was filled entirely with cattle. At the moment a bawling group was pushing into the shallow, swift-running mountain stream that bordered the valley as the pressure from the cows behind increased. Otherwise it was a comparatively calm herd, weary now after the long drive down from the foothills.

Dropping back down into his saddle, the Kid glanced across the flat at the riders he had sent around the herd's flank. He had three men to work with. Nate and the rest were at the Running H, pinning down Sven and his crew. As Dudley had hoped, Sven had been too complacent to leave anyone with the cattle overnight, since the herd was so close by his ranch. The Kid shook his head at such carelessness on the part of Torgeson. Dudley sure knew that cattleman's brand.

By the time this herd finished its run to Wild Horse Canyon, every fence in between would be a shambles. More important, when it was all over, at least half of Running H's stock would be gone, wiped out in one stroke.

The Kid caught sight of Tim pulling up on the far flank of the herd. Jimmy Blue and Frank were set on the other flank, ready to drive the herd away from the river toward the pass. The Kid stood up again in his stirrups and waved his hat. At once the crack of distant gunfire rattled along the valley's flanks.

The ground shook. The herd was off and running as one animal. His own gun out now and firing, the Kid galloped down the slope after the herd, amazed as always at the sudden, wild charge of a stampeding herd. The plunging backs were making straight for the entrance to the valley. They had plenty of room still, so there was no sound of clicking horns—just the thunder of their pounding hooves.

The Kid fired twice more over their backs, then holstered his weapon and hung on for the ride.

Sven pulled up. Ahead of him and slightly to his left had come the sudden, ominous rumble of a herd in swift motion. Without further thought he swung his horse to the left and galloped toward the sound. The rumbling grew deeper and soon swelled to a pitch that drowned out the sound of his own mount's pounding hooves.

He broke out from behind a clump of aspen and found

himself on the flank of his stampeding herd. He saw the dark, boiling mass stretching out in an irregular line, heading for the pass. Digging his spurs into his mount's flank, he shot forward in an effort to overtake the lead steers and turn them. As he raced alongside, the valley entrance loomed. The herd began to squeeze together. He heard the click of horns. His gun was out now and he was firing at a dozen burly steers in the lead, slowly turning them.

Working closer to the plunging backs, he swung up his six-gun and fired in the face of the lead steer. It bucked and swerved away, maddened. From the far side of the herd, then, a rider Sven recognized opened fire and the cattle swerved back at Sven. Immediately, Sven sent three quick shots at the lead steers. Obedient to their unleashed fear, they swerved back away from Sven, and Sven found himself overtaking the leaders, pulling in front. His horse felt strong under him. He cut. The lead animals began to turn.

At once, however, Sven felt pressure from another bunch coming at him from the other side. Glancing over his shoulder, Sven saw that the herd was now funneling together as it neared the pass. The herd could not be turned now, he realized. It was too late. He had run out of room. For all intents and purposes, he was now leading the stampede through the pass. His horse, aware of the thundering mass converging behind him, lifted to a tremendous, ground-devouring gallop. Sven heard gunfire behind him and felt the herd surging still closer to his mount's flying heels.

He swept on through the pass and out of the valley, the herd thundering after him. Ahead lay Indian Flats and, beyond that, Wild Horse Canyon. For one terrible sick moment he realized what these men intended. They were going to rimrock his herd—send this entire body of maddened cattle plunging off into that canyon!

Sven bent low over his horse. He had one chance. Now that he was out of the valley, he might be able to turn the leader. Twisting about in his saddle, he fired repeatedly at the lead steers. He saw one brute fall, but the bellowing and the fury only seemed to rise higher. There was a milling and grunting and bawling as cattle piled up, wave after wave on the downed steer's body, then rushed on. His gun's hammer snapped on an empty cylinder. Sven swore bitterly and holstered the useless six-gun.

Behind him now the firing from Slash D's men increased. Sven knew he was beaten. He would have to pull back if he didn't want to go over with his herd. Checking his horse, he swung away and loped out of the path of the cattle, then turned to watch the herd flow past, a helpless rage choking him.

He saw a line of fence go down before the charging cattle. It did not slow the rampaging herd for a second. There was no more gunfire from Slash D's men now, and Sven could make out no other riders beyond the plunging backs of his cattle as he kept pace with the stampede. Abruptly, a shoulder of rock loomed on his right. The flowing wedge turned to avoid the rock. Then Sven saw it happen. One side of the herd dropped off into the canyon as if they had been sheared away. The rest kept on, following the leaders over the lip, moving at full tilt. Some tried to stop but were bowled over. The cattle following, flowing blindly around them, seemed to float off the edge.

A dark river of swarming backs and clicking horns, they plunged to their deaths—until, abruptly, there were no more cattle left. The dust of their passage lifted into the gathering night, and, instead of the soul-shattering thunder of their hooves, Sven heard the feeble bawling of those cattle still alive at the foot of the drop. He rode to the rim and looked down. He could stand only one brief, sickening look before he hauled his horse back around; the bottom of the canyon was a struggling, boiling mass of dead and injured cattle.

He was so angry he felt light-headed. He knew what he must do. He must see to it now that Zach make good his promise to request a U.S. deputy marshal be sent in. Sven had recognized one of the Slash D riders stampeding his herd and would not hesitate to testify against him.

As he rode away from the sad, bawling tumult behind him, he saw a group of horsemen approaching through the gathering dusk. He recognized them instantly—Slash D riders every one, with Kid Bunning in the lead. For the first time his anger became tempered with caution—and fear. He had just witnessed what these men had done to a herd of dumb beasts. And he knew how much compunction these same men would feel in sending him over the rim as well. He pulled up nervously, aware that the six-gun on his hip was still empty.

Earlier, his eyes on the plunging sea of backs just in front of him, the Kid had been surprised to catch sight of Sven Torgeson galloping on the herd's flank. He had seen the rancher's futile attempts to turn the cattle and had been amused at the way he had been trapped in front of the herd as it boiled out through the pass.

For a while he began to hope the herd would overtake the fool, pound him into the ground. Who the hell would there be to point a finger? For some damn reason the herd had stampeded, killing the Running H owner. And that would be that. There might be a few cold stares when he and his boys rode into town. But that wouldn't last long. The Kid had long since learned that the so-called decent people of this earth had a very short memory when a silver dollar was spinning on a counter in front of them. Then the Kid saw Sven pull away from in front of the herd, defeated. The Kid frowned. He did not like that. Now they had a problem. Sven was a witness.

Suddenly, as if by magic, the herd began to disappear ahead of him. In a surprisingly short time the herd had flowed over the rim, and now the ground was still, the only sound the distant, feeble bawling of those cattle that had somehow survived the plunge.

The Kid took a deep breath, holstered his weapon, and pulled up. Lifting his hat off his head, he waved his men closer. Faces grimy, they trotted over, looking tired but grimly satisfied. The Kid nodded to them in appreciation for a job well done.

"Looks like we had one silly jasper trying to turn that herd," he remarked to the circle of riders.

"It was Torgeson," Tim said. "I think he recognized me, Kid."

"Damn fool should have been back with the rest of his people," the Kid replied coldly. "Wonder how the hell Nate let him get loose."

The Kid nudged his horse through the semicircle of riders, heading toward the canyon. The riders fell in behind him.

"Where we going?" Tim asked nervously.

The Kid looked back at Tim. "To take care of that witness, Tim, less'n you want him testifying all over this valley that he saw you rimrocking his cattle. Dudley made it pretty clear. He don't want no witnesses to what we just done."

The Kid swung back around in his saddle and rode on through the dusk toward the canyon, the others bunched behind him. He could feel the heavy displeasure in their manner. They had come to destroy a herd, not hunt down and kill a man in cold blood. Well, all they needed was to be tempered; it wouldn't take them long. Once they say how easy it was put out a man's lights, they'd take to it like a redskin to firewater.

And if they didn't, they'd better. This night's work was only the beginning.

For a moment Sven seriously considered spurring his horse back along the length of the canyon's rim. But that would be unabashed flight. That would be showing his heels to these butchers. Sven straightened his back and rode toward them, his face hard, his eyes filled with scorn.

The Kid pulled up first. As if by sleight of hand, his gleaming Smith & Wesson appeared in his fist. Sven saw the others draw their weapons also. But it seemed to Sven they did so reluctantly.

Sven pulled up. "You men can put your weapons away, if you dare," he told them. "My gun is empty, and I haven't had time to load it."

Some of the riders looked sheepishly at each other. One of them dropped his six-gun into his holster. This was the rider Sven had recognized. His name was Tim, he recalled.

"Evening, Tim," Sven said, nodding curtly to the man.

The fellow frowned and looked swiftly away from Sven's gaze. Abruptly, the Kid holstered his own weapon. As the rest of the riders followed suit, Sven felt enormous relief flood over him.

Then he saw the Kid lean forward and lift a rope from below his saddle horn. Before Sven could swing away, the rope had snaked out of the dusk, settling over his shoulders. Sven attempted to lift off the rope, but a vicious yank snugged it securely about his chest, pinning his arms. In that same moment, the crowd of horsemen rushed him.

Silently, they galloped beyond him, and a moment later he was hauled from his saddle. He began to twist in mid-air, then came down hard on his back. Barely conscious, he felt himself being dragged over the ground. A boulder embedded in the soil rose under him, raking him from his shoulder blade to his buttocks. He felt himself turning slowly, his face now plowing heedlessly through the torn-up ground.

He tried to free his arms so he could grab at the rope. But his senses were reeling. Was that a face he saw peering back at him through the dust? He thought he was near the canyon's rim, but couldn't be sure. Abruptly, the ground under him fell away. He heard a distant shout from above him. He twisted slowly, easily and saw, rushing up at him, the backs of still struggling animals. It reminded him of an immense pot of squirming armyworms. A split second before he struck, he caught sight of a downed steer tossing his horned head. As he felt the brute's horn explode deep inside his chest, his last thought was not of the riders galloping along the ridge, but of his daughter.

Sue! What would become of her!

Nine

ZACH HAD BEEN FEELING pretty grim since he left the Bar B's ramshackle impersonation of a working ranch. But now, at sight of Ty Simpson's Singletree ranch, he felt even worse.

The sprinkling of fresh green grass about the yard helped some, but it was not difficult for Zach to imagine how poorly this place would look under the merciless glare of a midsummer's sun. Two Mexican hands were repairing a sagging corral. They barely glanced up as Zach rode past. They were attempting to lift a heavy pole into place and lash it with rawhide and swearing a lot in the process.

Zach left his horse in some shade on the far side of the shack that served as the main ranchhouse. When he rounded the corner of the shack, he saw a tall, rangy fellow with red hair and a pale, drooping mustache. He was wearing boots, Levi's, a blue denim shirt, and a buttonless vest. His red hair was rumpled, his eyes puffy. Zach guessed that his unexpected arrival had awakened the fellow from a nap.

"The boss around?" Zach asked.

"Who'd that be?" The man seemed puzzled.

"Ty Simpson."

"Oh, sure. That's me."

"I'm the Flying T's new owner," Zach explained, "and I'd like to have a talk with you—about Dudley Stuart."

"What about the son of a bitch?"

"Could we go inside, out of this heat?"

"Sure. But it ain't much better inside."

Simpson turned and led the way into the house. Zach found himself in a single, cluttered room that stank of unwashed clothes and fried food. Simpson headed for a dishevled cot along one wall and left it to Zach to clear a seat for himself on a chair that held an old boot and a half-filled can of whitewash. Zach dropped the boot to the floor, then placed the can of whitewash on the floor carefully beside it and sat down.

Reaching under his cot, Simpson hooked a finger into a crockery jug and lifted it to his lips. Tipping back, he took a couple of large swallows, then handed the jug to Zach. "Have a drink and set a spell," he said. "Didn't know anybody was workin' the Flying T. Thought some whore owned it."

Zach took the jug, braced himself, and gulped down a decent swig. He gagged slightly as he lifted down the jug and handed the coffin varnish back to Simpson.

"Who did you say you was?" Simpson asked.

"I didn't," Zach said. "I'm Zach Stuart."

"Hey, you ain't no relation to *Dudley* Stuart, is you?"

"I am his son."

The man paled. "Well, Jesus. I'm sorry what I called your old man. You'll just have to remember he gave me no by-your-leave when he run roughshod over my range all these years." He frowned then and leaned close. "Hell, I never knowed Dudley *had* a kid."

Zach smiled thinly. "He didn't, either. Anyway, I've ridden out here to ask you to stand with me—and the Small Ranchers Association—against Dudley Stuart."

"*Against* Dudley?"

"That's right."

Simpson shook his head emphatically. "I ain't going against Dudley. He is one mean sonofabitch, and that's the truth. When he says shit, I squat, mister. He can use me any way he wants, just so he doesn't run me clean off my ranch. I'll get by. I never figured to get rich punchin' cows. That's for the big boys—like Dudley."

"Together, I figured we could stop Dudley Stuart from riding roughshod over small ranchers such as yourself. Isn't that what you'd like, Simpson?"

Again the man was emphatic. "Not on your life. That man can't be tamed none. He's best left to roam free, the way I see it. And besides, you should be more respectful of your old man, anyway. Hell, that spread of his will all be yours someday, won't it?"

Zach stood up. There was no sense in talking further with Ty Simpson. Zach had known that when he rode into the compound. His experience with the Bar B had been similar—only over there it had been the ranch owner's wife who had done all the talking. It was surprising how much she had sounded like Ty Simpson just now.

"Thanks for the drink, Ty."

"No sense in running off," the man said with absolutely no conviction. He pushed himself erect and stood there. He was obviously not going to walk Zach to the door.

Zach nodded his goodbye, turned on his heels, and left the house. Grateful to find himself back out in the bright spring sunshine, he walked briskly to his horse, mounted up, and rode from the ranch.

Zach was almost at the crest of a low ridge a good couple of miles from the Singletree when he noticed a rider approaching. At first he thought the rider was heading toward the Singletree until he saw him change direction slightly so as to bring himself into Zach's path.

Zach reined in his mount to give it a chance to blow, and waited for the rider to reach him. He recognized the man. It was Tobe Winston, Stirrup's foreman. When at last the scrawny, red-faced old timer pulled up alongside him, he chucked his battered Stetson wearily back off his forehead and considered Zach out of coolly appraising eyes. His white hair, straggling down from under his hat, lifted lightly in the soft breeze.

"You are a mean one to go chasin', and that's a fact," Tobe said. "That female tarantula at the Bar B didn't want to cooperate none at all. Said she didn't know which way you went after you left there. Said she didn't want to know. But her poor, sufferin' sonofabitch of a husband took his life in his hands and ventured the opinion you might be headed this way."

Zach smiled through his frown. "What's up, Tobe? Why are you out searching after me?"

The man's thin face went grim, his eyes flinty. "Some of Dudley's boys pulled out all the stops this time, Zach. They rimrocked Running H's entire spring herd."

Zach was startled. Dudley had come out of corner with a vengeance. "That's terrible, Tobe. We'll have to chip in, all of us, do what we can to restore Sven's herds. We can't let Dudley get away with something like this."

"Sven's dead, Zach. His men found him at the bottom of Wild Horse Canyon. He had gone over after his herd and landed on a critter's horn. It wasn't pretty and no one let Miss Sue see him. He was buried yesterday in a closed casket. We all chipped in."

"Let's hear the rest of it, Tobe."

Tobe told Zach of the attack on the Running H's compound. The way everyone figured, Sven must have come up, heard the firing, and ridden back to check on the herd. From the tracks on the canyon rim and the rope they found around Sven, it was pretty clear what had happened after that. Slash D's men had roped him and dragged him over the rim.

"There's no doubt then—" said Zach when Tobe finished.

"None at all."

"I think we better to see this Sheriff Pike. I don't care how much he owes Dudley, he can't look the other way after this."

"Hell, Zach. Like we told you before, Pike's in Dudley's back pocket. He's been lookin' the other way for years."

"Not after something like this, Tobe. At least, I'd like to see it if he does."

Tobe smiled thinly. "All right then. So why don't we ride back to Canyon City and find out for sure?"

"That's a good idea," Zach agreed grimly.

A moment later, riding alongside Tobe, Zach remembered Sue Torgeson standing at the door and telling him urgently that the ranchers in this valley were not a part of his vendetta.

Did she think so now? he wondered.

Zach found the county sheriff in the Long Spur next door to the lawman's office. He was at a back table concentrating grimly on a poker hand when Zach and Tobe pulled up beside him. To Zach he looked like the ruin of a lean and rawburned figure, a man who must once have commanded respect simply by the force of his personality. He was such a person no longer. His jowly face sagged, his skin was pale, his nose peeling from too much John Barleycorn. The paunch that flowed over his gunbelt completely obscured his buckle.

The sheriff suddenly flung down his cards and ran a meaty hand down over his face. As he leaned restlessly back in his chair, Zach said quietly, "We'd like to talk to you, Sheriff."

"Later," the man barked as he leaned forward to gather in a new hand.

Zach and Tobe had ridden well into the previous night. Only when they had become too exhausted to ride any further had they dismounted and made camp. They were up at dawn. Then, fortified only with coffee and what was left of Zach's jerky, they had ridden through the morning glare to Canyon City. Now it was past noon. The men had not eaten. They had gone directly to the sheriff's office as soon as they rode in. Zach was tired, and he knew Tobe was exhausted, also, though the old-timer had doggedly kept pace with him without a murmur.

"This is important, Sheriff," Zach said carefully. "Tobe

and I have ridden a long ways to see you."

"Shit," Pike said, studying his cards critically, "this here *game* is important, too! Sit down, sonny. I'll be with you when I finish here." He chuckled softly and discarded a card, puffing contentedly on his stogie. He seemed to have an idea his luck had changed.

It had. Zach kicked his chair out from under him.

Pike's hands flew up and his cards flew. His burly figure came down clumsily on the floor, the back of his head cracking sharply. In dazed fury, Pike clawed for his weapon. Zach stepped closer, waited for the gun to appear in his hand, then coolly kicked it out of Pike's grasp.

"Get up, Pike," Zach said mildly. "I figure now that you're finished here, we can go next door to your office and talk."

The burly lawman's fury abated slowly. He was on his back, weaponless. Cursing with a deadly earnestness, he got slowly to his feet, then reached back down to the floor for his hat. As he placed it back onto his head, he fixed Zach with a mean stare.

"You ain't heard the last of this."

"Don't expect I have." said Zach agreeably.

Someone handed the sheriff his weapon; he took it with an angry swipe and plunged it into his holster and shouldered his way out into the early afternoon sunlight. He did not look back at Zach or Tobe until he was inside his office.

"Tell me what's on your mind, then get out," Pike said, leaning back into his swivel chair.

Zach looked at Tobe. "Tell the sheriff what happened, Tobe."

When Tobe had finished, the sheriff was still slumped in his chair, a bored look on his face. "Hell," he said wearily. "I heard about that stampede. Everyone in town knows about that by this time. You think that's news to me?"

"Tobe says he knows who did it," Zach said. "Slash D riders. There were tracks on the rim, showing Sven was dragged by a rope and flung into the canyon. The rope was still around him when he was found."

"Sure. But how do you know it was Slash D riders done that?"

Tobe spoke up then. "More than one of the Running H's crew spotted Slash D men shooting up the compound that evening. Me and Zach figure that was a diversion."

"All that proves is the Slash D hands are lousy shots," Pike said. "Not a person got nicked, as I understand it. Just a few of Dudley's boys lettin' off steam 'cause of all them wires you fellows been stringing. How can you prove there's a connection? And I mean proof that'll stand up in a court of law?"

"Then you don't plan to do anything?" Zach asked.

"No, I don't. Not unless I get better evidence than this old buzzard's say-so."

Tobe looked at Zach. "See that, Zach? You believe me now? Your Pap owns this here tub of lard, lock, stock, and bellyful."

Zach looked with contempt back at the sheriff. "Yeah, Tobe. You're right. Let's get out of here."

As the two men left, the town constable hustled in past them, obviously anxious to get the sheriff's account of what just happened in the Long Spur. Tobe grunted as he watched the man disappear into the sheriff's office.

"And there goes Pike's toady. Wally and Pike. They make quite a pair. That's the law we got in this valley, Zach; and it sure ain't going to do us a whole hell of a lot of good."

Zach nodded. He could do what he promised the ranchers: see about having a deputy U.S. marshal sent in here. But that would take time. Too much time. No. Events would have to force such an action, and since Dudley had made the first move, it was up to the Association to make *its* move.

Zach and Tobe reached their horses. As Zach swung wearily into his saddle, he looked over at Tobe. "Ride for Stirrup, Tobe. Tell your boss there'll be a meeting of the association at my place tomorrow night. I'd like to see Sullivan there."

Tobe nodded grimly and hauled his horse away from the hitch rail. "See you then," he said, lifting his horse to a lope as he headed out of town.

Cookie had made plenty of coffee and two huge platters of doughnuts. Bill Handler sat beside Zach at the head of the table, looking around the near-empty kitchen hopefully. So far, only Sullivan and Tobe had shown up. Small talk had been exhausted. Sullivan, his black, bushy eyebrows knit with concern, explained that for the third time that he had been assured by a Diamond Cross rider that Dave Snyder planned to make this meeting.

Then came the pounding of hooves, followed soon after by the creaking of a buggy. The four men went to the kitchen door with Zach, who saw at once what had taken Snyder so long. The rancher was on horseback, escorting a buggy driven by Sue Torgeson, with Mary Snyder sitting beside her on the front seat. In the darkness, Sue was like a pale flower surrounded by dark petals in her somber mourning dress. She was helped down by Dave Snyder. Mary had stepped down herself before her husband had dismounted. The grim rancher's wife ducked into the ranchhouse past Zach and the others, her face pinched, her eyes cold.

Zach waited to greet Sue in the doorway. She allowed him to express his condolences with a surprising lack of bitterness in her eyes as she gazed back at him. Zach had been ready to accept the fact that when next she saw him, she might want to lash out and blame him for her father's death. But he saw now that the girl was made of better stuff than that.

Which only made him feel worse.

As soon as everyone had settled in, Zach tapped the meeting to order.

"I called this meeting," he said, "so we could discuss what action we should take in retaliation for what Dudley has done. If anyone has any suggestions, I am sure the rest of us would like to hear them."

Zach leaned back then and listened as everyone offered plans of one sort or another. Sullivan wanted to do to Dudley's herds what he had done to the Running H's herds. Sue was bitter when she learned what Sheriff Pike's response had been. Tobe thought it might be a good idea to see if they could get the merchants of Canyon City to refrain from selling any more goods to the Slash D, a boycott in reverse. This was almost immediately discarded, however, when Sullivan pointed out how indebted to Dudley most of those merchants were.

At last Zach cleared his throat. "I think," he said quietly, "we must retaliate not in kind, but in such a way that we will really restrict Dudley's operations in the future."

"What have you got in mind?" asked Mary Snyder sharply, her lips compressed angrily.

Surprised at her joining into the discussion so forcefully, Zach said, "Mary, Dudley needs water for his livestock now more than ever. He can't get to his usual water holes without cutting across land that is no longer his. He has Indian Springs and the Little Whiskey. I propose to take Indian Springs from him."

"How?" she asked, her eyes glinting.

"I have a plan."

"Good," she snapped. "I hope it works. Take Indian Springs from Dudley." Then Mary looked around the table at the others. "I really don't care what the rest of you think of it. But Dave and I think Zach should do it. With Zach and Dudley at each other's throats, I don't see why both of them won't sooner or later be frying in hell! And the sooner, the better."

Zach heard Sue gasp. Dave appeared thunderstruck by his wife's words.

Mary stood up and looked down at Sue. "Are you coming, Sue?" she asked.

She was out the door before any of them could protest, Sue jumping up to hurry after her. As Dave Snyder also scrambled to his feet, he looked quickly back at the others. "I—I guess I'll let you men decide how to go about it."

And then he too was gone.

As the sound of Sue's buggy faded in the night, Tobe grinned. "Phew!" he said, taking out a large blue handkerchief and mopping his brow comically.

Grinning, Zach turned to Cookie. "We better have them doughnuts now," he said. "And pass around the coffee, too."

"Good idea," said Sullivan, grinning also, as he brought out his flask. "Looks like we got some planning to do."

Zach looked at Sullivan. "Tell me about Indian Springs first. I want to know how exposed it is."

"What have you got in mind?"

"I'll tell you when you give me a clear picture of the place."

Sullivan chuckled and poured a healthy dollop of whiskey into his steaming coffee. Zach reached for one of Cookie's doughnuts. He wished he felt as much like chuckling as Sullivan did. But it was pretty difficult, with Mary's words hanging in the air like a curse.

Ten

INDIAN SPRINGS WAS A small, ramshackle community high in the mountains back of the Slash D. The year-round spring that gave the place its name bubbled from a cleft high on a slope above the town amidst a field of colossal, slablike formations that stuck out of the ground like the headstones of some deceased race of Titans.

When Dudley Stuart had first entered the valley, he had damned the flow leading from the springs, creating a large reservoir well above the town, from which a much heavier stream was created to feed into the flats below the town, providing a lush, summer-round growth. The long grass and ample water enabled Dudley to pasture a large portion of his herds. It was still his best pasture thoughout the summer months and well into the autumn.

The town itself was no more than a shabby collection of buildings on a bare, stump-pocked piece of tableland below the reservoir flanking a rutted logging road that cut with startling straightness through the valley. There was a big saloon, a general store and a blacksmith shop. Not much farther up the road there was an unpainted hotel of frame construction. Its sides had weathered poorly over the years with much of the siding now warped and blistered. The porch looked positively unsafe.

The Kid noted all this with a single glance as he rode into town beside Nate, the two of them at the head of five

Slash D riders. He had only a vague idea what he was doing riding into this sorry excuse for a town, but he knew it had something to do with a rider that had galloped into the Slash D compound late the night before.

The Kid remembered Nate, in answer to a summons from Felicia soon after, cursing sleepily and plunging out blindly into the chill spring night, hastily pulling on his Levi's.

Nate had not been very helpful at breakfast. He seemed almost as puzzled as the Kid by his orders to ride out to Indian Springs and guard the place.

"From what, Nate?" the Kid had asked, mopping his plate clean with a corn muffin.

"From Zach Stuart, and the rest of them ranchers."

"How does Dudley know he's gonna attack there?"

"Dudley didn't say. But he knows."

And that was where it stood now. Zach had a turncoat in his camp, which would make things mighty interesting from here on in. But Nate didn't know exactly *when* the attack was supposed to take place. Dudley had just told him to hole up in the town and keep a watch around the clock.

Throughout the long ride up here, the Kid had kept his mouth shut. It was close to noon now, and as they dismounted in front of the saloon, he glanced at Nate. "Did you get a chance to see who that was who rode in last night?"

Nate shook his head. "Nope. The rider was gone by the time I got to the ranchhouse."

The Kid shrugged and followed Nate into the saloon. He was parched.

Zach was not pleased. The Running H and the Diamond Cross had counted themselves in, but it was Zach's men, mostly, and a few of Sullivan's crew who were carrying this operation. Sullivan, because of his avowed expertise in dealing with explosives, was coming up on the springs from the other side of the ridge, well above Indian Springs, with a wagon load of dynamite. It would be Sullivan himself who would set the charges.

Sullivan had assured Zach that the granite outcropping surrounding the springs could be brought down easily. But Sullivan would have to have the time to drill the needed blowholes in the sides of the granite, unless he could find cracks already large enough and deep enough.

All that, Zach understood only vaguely. The important thing, from his point of view, was that Sullivan knew what he was doing and needed time to do it. This last was where Zach came in. He would lead his contingent into Indian Springs and take the town over as quietly as possible, then move up the slope to back Sullivan's play. It was inconceivable to Zach that Dudley would not have at least a few men at the springs, guarding them and the reservoir. Zach and Sullivan had made camp together for the evening meal, then Sullivan had ridden off into the night with Tobe Winston driving, somewhat nervously, the wagon containing the dynamite.

It was late the following afternoon now and Zach was in sight of the town. About this time, it had been planned, Sullivan, on the other side of the ridge, should be in sight of the springs. He would be waiting for Zach to move up from the town and flush any Slash D men that might be guarding them.

Zach glanced at Bill Handler. "Let's go, Bill."

Bill turned to look back at the men. "We'll just ride in nice and casual," Bill told them. "No sense in causing a commotion, unless we have to."

The men nodded.

They settled into an easy trot, the riders strung out along the narrow dirt road, the town's buildings growing steadily clearer in the bright mountain air. It took less than ten minutes to reach the outskirts of the settlement. The single hotel loomed before them first, a two-story frame dwelling with warped siding. There was no activity about it, Zach noted. Indeed, the entire town resembled a ghost town. He glanced at Bill, riding beside him.

"Looks pretty quiet, don't it."

"Too damn quiet," Bill admitted. The foreman pulled his holster around so it rested higher on his thigh.

They rode on past the hotel. Zach could understand why no one would be rocking on its porch. It could not carry the weight of a full-grown man. Some windows on the third floor were boarded up.

There were five horses at the rail in front of the saloon, two more in front of the blacksmith shop across the street from it, and three more in front of the general store next door.

Yet not a soul appeared on the street. No one drifted across. No one was leaving a store. No one sat on a porch. And the blacksmith shop seemed curiously silent: the clangor of the smithy's hammer still, despite the presence of two customers within, if the evidence of those two horses meant anything.

"I don't like it," said Zach to Bill suddenly. "Tell the boys to spread out."

Bill swung his horse around and rode back toward the rest of the men. Zach nosed his mount toward the hitch rail in front of the saloon. He was dismounting when the first shot was fired.

It came from behind the blacksmith shop. The round whistled noisily through the space where his head had been. Zach's gun was out and he was driving for the saloon, when two men appeared in the doorway, six-guns blazing.

Zach darted around the corner of the saloon and hotfooted it toward the back. A rapid fusilade followed him, slugs whining like angry hornets past his shoulder. Just before he reached the rear of the saloon, a figure stepped out from behind the privy and fired point-blank at Zach.

Why the bullet missed, Zach had no idea. He flung

himself to the ground, rolled over once, and then steadied himself long enough to get off a clear shot. His assailant was standing in full view, his back to the privy, his six-gun tracking the tumbling Zach.

Both men fired at the same time.

But it was Zach's round which stamped a neat hole in the gunman's blue cotton shirt, the force of the slug slamming the man back against the privy wall. Somehow, he managed to steady himself against the wall and bring up his six-gun a second time. Zach sighted carefully on the man's chest and fired. This round punched a hole alongside the other one, its force driving the man sideways. As his hand dropped, his gun discharged into the ground at his feet. Then he sagged slowly to the ground.

Zach heard someone racing along the alley that led from the hotel. He scrambled to his feet and ducked behind the privy, keeping it between him and the saloon as he reloaded. Then he poked his head out and saw Bill, his .44 smoking, running toward him.

"You all right, Zach?" he cried, ducking behind the privy.

"Not a scratch," Zach said. "How's it going?"

"Just as I got the fellows to pull up so they could scatter some, the fireworks began. We got two holed up in the hotel, and I think Pierre's been hit, only it ain't serious, judging from the way he's been cursing." He frowned angrily about him. "We rode right into an ambush, Zach!"

"I figured that, Bill."

Sporadic firing came from back up the street—the hotel, most likely. Closer, Zach heard the saloon window shattering, and a shout coming from the inside.

"I guess," said Bill, "they were waiting for us to walk into the saloon. Figured we'd go there first to slake our thirst. But when they saw us slow down and maybe getting suspicious, that jasper from behind the blacksmith shop opened up on you. We caught him and them two others that tried to cut you down. There's another one still inside the saloon, and, as near as I can gather, them two we got in the hotel is about all we got to worry about now. Down here, that is."

"Take Thompson and Manny. Clean out the hotel. Send Pierre back here with me and tell the rest to listen and make their move on the saloon when I do. Pierre and I will be blasting in from the back."

Zach finished loading his Colt as Bill hurried back down the alley. In a few moments Zach saw Pierre, carrying his rifle and limping slightly, hurrying toward him. Zach smiled. He had no intention of waiting for Pierre to reach him. He had just wanted to see the man running up the alley toward him, well out of the line of fire.

Zach darted out from behind the privy and burst through the saloon's rear door, crouching, his six-gun sweeping in a wide arc in front of him. Zach saw a shadowy figure at the window jump up and turn as he cleared the bar. A snap shot took the fellow's hat off. He promptly flung himself down behind an overturned table and began a rapid fire.

Bullets whined around Zach. A bottle behind him disintegrated. He ducked behind the end of the bar just as two of his men burst into the saloon. The man crouching behind the table flung his hands into the air, and it was over.

One of the men called out, "You all right, Zach?"

Coughing in the thick smoke, Zach replied that he was fine, and led the two men out the rear of the saloon. As one of them took the captured Slash D rider down the alley toward the hotel, Zach took the remaining fellow and started up the slope toward the springs, a disgruntled Pierre limping along just behind them.

"You ain't going to leave me behind this time," Pierre called.

Zach laughed and turned to wait for Pierre to catch up. "I figured you'd stopped enough lead already."

"You worry about yourself, Zach," said Pierre. "This here's just a flesh wound."

The three of them continued on up the slope. They passed the reservoir without incident and soon found themselves crossing a field strewn with enormous boulders. Beyond the field, the ground lifted sharply. The next hundred yards made it a real struggle for Pierre, and he was soon well in the rear. The slope eased and Zach saw that he was approaching an enormous pile of rock slabs. To his right, he saw the swift-running water, the icy stream that poured forth from Indian Springs. Zach pulled up to wait.

As soon as Pierre had joined them, they moved forward again, keeping low and using whatever cover offered itself.

"Hey!" said Pierre shortly, ducking his head swiftly.

Zach followed his gaze and saw three Slash D men positioned on a small bluff. They had rifles, and were in an excellent position to open up on anyone approaching the springs. A frontal attack up the slope would be suicide. Zach motioned to Pierre and his other man to keep down. So far, their arrival on the scene had gone unnoticed. Zach could only hope that somewhere on the other side of that bluff, well hidden, crouched Sullivan and Tobe, their wagonload of dynamite nearby.

Zach realized that the three had probably not been overly alarmed at the sound of gunfire coming from the town below. They would most likely have assumed it was simply their fellows springing that ambush.

A little to the right, Zach noted, there was a small clump of scrub pine. Just beyond the pine was a large boulder. From the boulder to the slope leading to the bluff was a short dash. He decided he would try it before those three on the bluff discovered what was up.

He turned to Pierre. "I want you to use that rifle the

way Cookie did not so long ago," he told him. "Cover me. But don't shoot until you see one of us is in trouble. We're going to storm that bluff."

Zach looked at the other fellow with him. He was a young sprout and he looked somewhat green around the gills. "Just keep low and follow me," Zach told him.

Zach darted the short distance to the pines, waited for the other to catch up, then left the pines and raced toward the boulder. Once behind it, he crouched low and waited for his companion to reach him. The man was sweating gumdrops by this time, but he was game.

"Ready?" Zach asked him.

The fellow nodded.

Zach darted out from behind the boulder and raced over the ground toward the steep slope leading to the bluff. The ground was thickly carpeted, and the two made barely a sound as they raced across the open ground. The three men on the bluff were intent on the far slope, which Zach assumed was where the springs originated. Abruptly, the two men came upon loose shale. Their boots clattered loudly as they raced along.

One of the three men turned and looked down at them. Zach heard the man's high, startled cry and saw the three turn and swing up their rifles. He didn't know whether to throw himself flat or just keep running.

He never had to make the decision. A mind-numbing blast shattered the air. Dynamite! Zach felt his ears pop and saw two of the men scrambling, dazed, off the bluff, their rifles gone. Only one of the men remained in sight, and he was on his hands and knees, groping blindly. Though the blast had shaken Zach, he regained his bearings enough to continue on up the slope. To his dismay, he saw that the man left on the bluff had found what he was groping for—his rifle. He had caught sight of Zach and now brought his rifle up to his shoulder.

From behind, Pierre's rifle cracked. The man on the bluff sagged, then pitched forward down the slope. A moment later Zach and his companion were standing on the bluff. Through the dust and debris still sifting down from the blast, Zach grinned at Ken Sullivan, who was standing beside a boulder some distance down the slope.

"What the hell kept you?" Sullivan called up.

Before Zach could answer, he heard the faint thunder of hooves from far below. Squinting through the late-afternoon sunlight, he saw three riders galloping from Indian Springs, heading south toward the Slash D. A second or two later two others followed. Then Zach caught sight of Bill Handler and the rest of his men racing up the slope past the reservoir toward them.

The sound of gunfire, plus the blast, had prompted Bill and the others to forget their siege of the hotel and race up the slope to join Zach.

Zach turned and looked back down at Sullivan and saw him approaching Tobe at the foot of the slope. Tobe was driving the wagon out from behind some rocks. He waved up to Zach. Calling to Pierre and the others to follow, Zach started down the steep incline to see if he could give Sullivan a hand with planting the dynamite.

As he scrambled down the slope, a nagging, unpleasant thought plucked at the back of his mind. This operation had almost failed. Two men were dead because someone had warned Dudley of Zach's intention to attack Indian Springs.

Who was it?

Before they made any more plans together, they would have to find out.

The thing to do now was to blow the spring *and* the dam holding back the reservoir—then get the hell out of there, fast! Luckily, it would be a moonless night when they rode back across Slash D land.

Eleven

A WEARY, ALMOST RESIGNED Dudley Stuart pulled his horse about and left the mean hillside cemetery where he had just finished burying the two men who had died defending Indian Springs from his son's assault. The assault had dealt him a crippling blow, and so had the deaths of the two Slash D riders. He had known the men only in passing and neither had made much of an impression on him. Yet they had pledged their allegiance and loyalty to the outfit the moment they threw their bedroll into the Slash D chuck wagon; and Dudley knew that he owed them for that loyalty, seeing as how they had given their lives—as mean and unpromising as they might have been—as a mark of their fealty.

He owed them and he owed himself.

Nate and Kid Bunning were riding behind him. The remainder of his crew, with the exception of those who were still filling in graves, were trailing along behind. Dudley knew from their looks that there was not a single one of them who would not back him with enthusiasm if he told them to ride on Zach's Flying T that very moment. They would willingly join him in razing every building, killing every man—including Zach.

Yes, they would take special delight in killing Zach. Dudley could see the Kid licking his chops even now at the prospect.

Indian Springs loomed ahead. Beyond it, well down

the road, Dudley saw a lone rider on his way toward them. He squinted through the bright morning sunlight and recognized the man.

Marty Pike.

Which meant, sure as bears shit in the woods, there was trouble. Bad trouble. It would take something like that to get the county sheriff off his fat ass and away from a poker table.

As Dudley and his riders clattered into Indian Springs, the hoofbeats of their horses echoed hollowly in the deserted town. The only one left in the place was the blacksmith, who stood now in the entrance to his shop, watching them ride past. He would stay on. Dudley had already given him permission. The man made his living from a very fine still he ran up in the hills, and Dudley had no intention of depriving himself of its product. He waved as he rode past. The blacksmith touched the brim of his broad-brimmed hat in return, then turned and vanished back inside his shop.

Just outside of town, Dudley came to the broad gulley scoured across the road by the sudden wash that resulted when Zach blew the damn. To Dudley's left, the flat resembled a swamp in springtime. The stream that had meandered through it had vanished. By midsummer the flat would be grazed out; and with no spring to feed it, it would simply burn in the hot midsummer sun.

On the other side of the gulley, Dudley pulled up to wait for the sheriff. His riders crowded about him, then nudged their horses back and away from him out of respect. Only Nate and the Kid remained close as the sheriff pulled up, chucked his hat back, and folded his arms over his pommel. Sweat was crawling down his face in large, dirty beads. He looked flushed from the exertion of the ride; his eyes were puffy from not enough sleep the night before.

He was Dudley's man; Dudley had bought him cheap. Glancing over him now, Dudley was not proud of his purchase.

"Jesus, Dudley," the lawman said, "what the hell's goin' on here, anyways? You got any idea what a stink this has raised in the capital?"

"I can imagine," Dudley replied drily.

"This has put me on the griddle, Dudley," he bleated, taking out a huge red handkerchief and mopping his brow. "And it's your fault!"

"How so?" Dudley asked, mildly surprised at his own patience in dealing with this swollen mistake for a lawman. "It was none of my doing. Zach rode in here with his men and destroyed the springs and the dam I had built. In the process, he killed two of my men and severely wounded four others." He smiled coldly at Pike. "Seems to me you should be confronting Zach about now with that complaint you just hurled at me."

Dudley could see the sheriff catch himself. He was aware suddenly that he had spoken to Dudley without caution, and with precious little respect. Dudley, he realized, was controlling himself with some difficulty. It would not take much to push the rancher over the edge. With a quick glance at the Kid, then at Nate, Pike moistened his dry, alkali-caked lips, and tried to smile.

"Now, it ain't that I'm blamin' you, Dudley. But you got to see my side of it. The newspapers in the capital have called this a full-scale range war. The attorney general wants me to request a deputy U.S. marshal to ride in here and put a lid on things, if'n I can't manage it myself."

"What was your reply?"

"I ain't done that yet. That's why I been chasin' all over hell and beyond lookin' for you. I wanted to talk to you first, before I sent him a reply."

"You did fine, Pike." Dudley smiled coldly. "You telegraph that attorney general and tell him it was all a misunderstanding. You tell him everything's under control."

"You sure I can tell him that, Dudley?"

"I'll be sending a few telegrams myself, soon's I ride into Canyon City. I still got plenty of friends in the capital. This young attorney general, I don't know, but I'll see to him. He's just looking for headlines, I'm thinking." Dudley frowned. "I suppose *The Citizen*'s been blowing this thing out of all proportion, as well." *The Citizen* was Canyon City's own small daily.

"Sure. That's where them capital newspapers got the story."

Dudley nodded. "I'll go in and see Bellows. Remind him of a few IOU's." He smiled at Pike. "And don't worry, Pike. We'll keep the lid on things from here on in. Don't want no deputy marshal messin' around in Canyon City politics, do we?"

"We sure as hell don't, Dudley." The fat lawman seemed relieved.

"And one thing more, Pike," Dudley said softly, "the next time you speak to me in front of my men, I suggest you show more respect. I'm just not in the mood to sit still for your vomit. Now, you think you can remember that?"

"Oh, shit, Dudley," Pike cried, in a sudden panic, "you don't have to worry none about that." He was moping his face frantically again with the oversized handkerchief. "I was just excited is all. I'd been riding' since late yesterday when I got that telegram and I was plumb wore out."

"I would have stopped in to see you yesterday, but I was busy bringing in those men Zach wounded. Took the best part of the day to see to them. I only now got to buryin' the two he killed. I ain't been sittin' on my ass neither, Pike. About time you earned your keep."

Then, with a curt nod, Dudley nudged his horse on. His men rode contemptuously past the sheriff. Some flicked amused glances at him, but most did not even bother to acknowledge his presence.

Soon the lawman was at the rear of Slash D's riders, blinking unhappily through the dust their passage had raised.

Dudley Stuart's entrance into *The Citizen*'s place of business caused a mild stir. He was not alone. Just behind him strode Nate and the Kid. The men at the two presses stopped feeding them and turned to watch Dudley's progress as he pushed through the low gate and headed for the glassed-in office of the editor and publisher at the rear. Two other editors, busy at a high table setting up the day's front page, pulled back, wooden mallets still poised over the type.

Dudley nodded to them as he passed, his face grim, unsmiling. Glancing through the glass door, Dudley saw Bellows push his gold spectacles up onto his narrow forehead and get to his feet. He had been going over copy at his desk and had not seen Dudley, apparently, until this moment.

Dudley opened the door and strode in, Nate and the Kid following in behind him. "Hello, Sam," Dudley said. "Caught you at a bad time, did I?"

"As a matter of fact, I'm rushing to get the afternoon edition ready, Dudley. Can this wait?" He looked nervously at Nate and the Kid, who were standing with their arms folded, their backs resting lightly against the glass wall.

"I'm afraid it can't, Sam," said Dudley, sitting down in the wooden, straight-backed chair. He took off his hat and placed it carefully on the edge of the newspaperman's desk.

Bellows leaned back in his chair. "I'd appreciate it if you'd make it brief then, Dudley."

"No problem with that," Dudley responded, smiling. "I just want you to calm down your front page some—about this range war you've been proclaiming. It is getting my friends in the capital nervous, Sam. Hell, this ain't no range war." Dudley smiled gently. "It's just a family quarrel."

The publisher's narrow face went pale. "You're not telling me to soft-pedal what's been going on, are you, Dudley? I did what I could to hush up that terrible business at The Belle Fourche; but that, it seems, was only the beginning. This isn't any family quarrel, Dudley, and you know it."

"Now you listen to me, Sam," said Dudley, leaning

closer to the man, "and listen good. You like them poker sessions out at my place and the women I import. You also don't seem to mind none if I carry your IOU's. You are one lousy poker player, mister. Now you stop reporting all this nonsense or I'll call in that paper and find myself running this here rag." Dudley leaned back, picked up his hat, stood up, and looked coldly down at Bellows. "Do I make myself clear?"

Bellows swallowed. His glance flicked to Nate and the Kid. Then he looked up at Dudley with as much indignation as he could muster, his protruding Adam's apple bobbing frantically. "You're *threatening* me, Dudley!"

Dudley put his hat on and nodded curtly. "That's right, Bellows. I'm calling in my IOU's, you might say. And if that don't work—" He shrugged. "Well, I'll just let you use your imagination, Sam."

Dudley glanced at Nate and the Kid, then nodded curtly again. They turned and led the way out of the office. As Dudley paused to close the door behind him, he smiled down at the publisher.

"We'll have to postpone them poker sessions for a while, Sam," he said. "But as soon's this here family quarrel's over, we won't have no trouble getting a few of my friends out. I'll let you know when."

"Them—them IOU's, Dudley—" The man was perspiring.

"I could just tear them up, Sam. No reason for me to hold them over the head of a friend, I'm thinking."

Bellows swallowed, his color returning. "I'd sure appreciate that, Dudley."

"Rest easy, then. You know what I want."

Dudley pulled the door shut and left the place and found Nate and the Kid waiting on the sidewalk. Diagonally across the street, The Belle Fourche was going full blast.

The thought of that whore still operating in Canyon City after what she had done to him filled him with an icy fury. He had not counted on her being able to remain in this town after the calculated degradation he had personally heaped upon her. But it was plain that some women not only had no pride, but no soul, as well.

Well, he thought blackly, sooner or later he would meet her in Hell. There, he would finish with her.

Twelve

"WHAT HAPPENED WAS WE stood up to him," said Sullivan, glancing quickly about him, his eyes gleaming in triumph. "I don't see why we got to start wondering what he's up to. Seems to me it's obvious. He's pulling in his horns. He's already sold off a quarter of his herd, I hear tell."

Snyder leaned back, pleased, and waited for someone else to speak. This was another meeting of the Small Ranchers Association, and this time they were meeting in Zach's kitchen. Cookie hovered in attendance, and the room was bursting with the rich aroma of strong coffee and freshly baked doughnuts. The Bar B and the Singletree spreads were still not represented, but that didn't bother Zach. In attendance were Sue Torgeson for the Running H, Dave Snyder and his wife for the Diamond Cross, and Sullivan and Tobe Winston for Stirrup. Bill Handler was sitting beside Zach at the head of the table. Snyder was running the show, his wife sitting in a wooden chair against the wall behind him. Zach was sure Snyder could feel his woman's eyes on him. They were probably singeing the hair at the nape of his neck.

"It's been almost a month, I admit," said Zach cautiously. "And it does seem as if we've got Dudley on the run. I just wish we wouldn't get too sure of ourselves, though. Seems to me Dudley rolled over a mite easily."

Mary spoke up bluntly. "I don't think you *want* your

father to pull in his horns, Zach. That would not fit in with your plans."

"And what *are* my plans, Mary?"

"To destroy your father—wipe him out. Do you deny that? All of us here know what you told Dudley at the graveside of your mother."

"Now, Mary," protested Sullivan. "That's *his* business."

Mary snorted. "*Is* it, really? Hasn't Zach made it ours? Aren't we his tools in this scheme of his to bring down his father?"

"That's pretty harsh, Mary. Are you forgetting what Dudley's hired gunslicks did to Sue's father?"

"Please, Ken," broke in Sue. "Of course Mary is not forgetting that. How can any of us *ever* forget what happened to my father?" Sue turned then to face Mary. "It is not fair for us to blame Zach for our problem with Dudley, Mary. I admit I tried to do that, once. But it is dangerous to look anywhere but at Dudley Stuart for our troubles. And Zach is right. We must not get too sure of ourselves."

"I'm not so sure," Mary snapped. Then she leaned back in her chair, her eyes staring coldly across the table to Zach.

Snyder had looked very unhappy during this heated exchange. "Now, there's no reason for us to fight among ourselves," he said nervously. "Whatever the reason, Sullivan's right. Dudley Stuart has pulled in his horns, and I, for one, think we should take advantage of it."

"How?" asked Zach.

"Finish our fencing." He smiled. "Outside of that, business as usual. I don't need to tell you fellows what condition our pastures are in. I've never seen it better. Seems to me the tallow is pilin' on our beef at a fine rate."

The man was plainly jubilant with the outlook, and Zach was reluctant to say anything that would put a damper on his—or anyone else's—good spirits. Yet, he felt he owed it to these men to urge upon them one last precaution.

"All right," he said, "business as usual. But I suggest you keep a sharp eye out for trouble. It won't do any harm to be careful. Don't forget what happened to Running H's herd. I suggest night guards at every camp and certainly a night guard over your herds."

Ken frowned thoughtfully, then nodded. "I think that's a good idea," he said. "Won't do any harm at all to be careful."

There was general agreement to that.

"Well, if that's all," Snyder said, about to close the meeting, "I suggest we call—" Then he saw Zach's finger waving slightly. "Yes, Zach. What else?"

Zach cleared his throat. "Bill and I have been discussing this for some time, and we both figure we should bring it up here. It isn't a very pleasant topic, but I don't see how we can avoid it."

Snyder frowned. "What is it now, Zach?" The man was plainly weary of Zach's insistence on bringing up unpleasant matters. He was anxious to relax and enjoy the good times that had finally come to the valley.

"Bill and I agree that someone tipped our raid on Indian Springs. Slash D riders were waiting for us. Bill said it was Nate Claw and the Kid who were holed up in the hotel. They wouldn't have been waiting for us there unless they knew we were coming."

"Well, it didn't seem to stop you none," said Mary Snyder, still not finished with Zach, it seemed.

"There's two men dead because of that ambush. Our plan was to go in quietly, disarm what few Slash D riders might be there, then blow up the springs."

"Are you sorry you had to kill those men?" Mary snapped. "That surprises me."

"Of course, I am," Zach replied. "One of those men I had to kill myself. That was *not* part of our plan. The point is, it need not have happened, and it would not have happened if that raid on Indian Springs had not been tipped off in advance."

"That's a serious charge," said Sullivan. "You didn't mention this to me earlier."

"I know. Like I said, Bill and I have been discussing this for some time. You can understand why I am so reluctant to bring it up now. But I don't see what choice I've got. Someone on our side has gone over to Dudley."

"Surely," said Sue, "you don't mean to accuse any of us here!"

Zach hesitated. That hesitation was sufficient to make his point. There was a noticeable intake of breath around the table. Instantly, nervous glances shuttled from one to the other, and then, outrage on their faces, everyone turned on Zach.

"You can't mean that," insisted Sue. "One of *us?*"

"More'n likely one of the men's gone over," suggested Snyder hastily.

"I don't believe that's the answer," Zach said firmly.

"You mean you trust thirty-dollar-a-month cowpokes before you'd trust us?" Snyder asked angrily.

"Well," said Zach coldly, "I'm willing to speak for my riders, every last one of them."

"And I'll vouch for mine," said Sullivan. He fixed Snyder with a cold pair of eyes. "I didn't notice any of your men riding into Indian Springs with mine, Snyder," Sullivan reminded the owner of the Diamond Cross.

"I sent none of my men along with yours, Zach," Sue said tightly, her face flushed. "Does that mean you suspect—me or one of my riders?"

Zach shrugged. Snyder and his wife got swiftly to their feet. Sue followed their example. Sullivan let his gaze rest on all three, one at a time, his face grim. Zach saw that things were about to get ugly.

He cleared his throat. "No sense in getting all riled. There's always the chance that Dudley just guessed right in sending Nate Claw and the Kid to Indian Springs—

seeing as how trouble was brewing. After all, I did expect there'd be some of his riders on guard."

Everyone but Zach and Bill Handler exchanged glances. Zach saw the tension ease noticeably. There was still a threat of an explosion in the air. It reminded Zach of how it felt watching storm clouds building in the sky. But this time there was a slight break in the clouds. And soon it was obvious there would be no storm.

"Sit down, sit down," said Sullivan wearily. "No need to walk out in a lather. Sit down. Hell, maybe Zach's right. Maybe Dudley just guessed right. He could've, you know. He's that wily a man."

Snyder and his wife and Sue Torgeson sat down.

"We'll just have to be careful the next time we plan any joint action," said Zach.

"There won't be a next time," insisted Snyder. "Dudley's licked and there's an end to this business. And good riddance, I say."

"Amen!" said his wife ferverently.

"I think we'd better go now," said Sue. "I'm tired and it will be a long ride back to the Running H."

"You can stay with us," Mary Snyder suggested quickly.

"No," Sue said. "Not tonight. I want to get back."

Zach looked beyond Sue and saw the stricken look on Cookie's long, mournful countenance. He desperately wanted to show off his coffee and doughnuts. "At least stay for Cookie's doughnuts," Zach suggested.

Sue looked at Zach for a long moment. She tried to keep her face hard, her eyes cold; but almost against her will, it seemed, her expression softened. When Zach saw he had won, he smiled at Pete.

"Bring on the refreshments, Cookie. We've had enough business for one night."

Not long after, Zach and Bill Handler stood in the yard and watched the evening's guests ride off, with Mary and

Dave Snyder driving their spring wagon. In a moment the sound of their horses had faded and all that disturbed the quiet of the moonless night was the rattle of Cookie cleaning up in the kitchen.

Bill turned to Zach. "Who do you think it is, Zach?"

"I'm not sure, Bill. And before I am, I don't want to say. I could be wrong—and I sure hope I am. What I'm hoping now is whoever went to Dudley before won't dare try it a second time."

"I hope you're right," said Bill.

"And I hope Snyder's right—that there won't need to be another time, that Dudley really is finished."

"You hope it," said Bill, his eyes glinting in the light from the kitchen window. "But do you *believe* it?"

Turning to go back inside, Zach paused and looked around at his foreman. "No, Bill, I don't. Not by a damn sight. There's a storm brewing. I can feel it."

Zach continued on into the ranchhouse, thanked Cookie, then went into his bedroom and undressed for bed. He had spent a long day in the saddle. In the past three days he must have covered fifty miles on horseback as he checked out his fencing. And, like Dave Snyder, he was pleased at the speed with which his beef were putting on the tallow. His stock had been a mite stringy after it made the long trek from Texas, but this past month on good pasture had done wonders.

Zach lay back on his pillow, his arms crossed under his head. He saw in his mind's eye the valley's pastures filled with Flying T stock. This, then, was what it could be like to have a good spread. This was the old cowpoke's dream come true. But it was a dream that could turn nightmare at any moment.

Zach remembered his last words to Bill a moment before: *There's a storm brewing. I can feel it.*

Yes, he could feel it. The calm before the storm. But *was* that what he felt? Perhaps it was something else he felt. It might be that he was restless and anxious at the thought that his father actually was pulling in his horns and that from here on in there would be no more provocations, nothing to incite Zach to battle.

If that were to be, then what excuse would Zach have to confront his father and bring him down as he and Jane had planned and looked forward to for so long? By letting Zach—and the other ranchers—work their spreads in peace Dudley would be cheating his son of the vengeance he had promised himself all these years.

The fear that this was so, Zach realized, was nagging at him. This was the source of the tension he felt. The thought shamed him. Perhaps Sue Torgeson was right about him, after all.

Eyes wide now as he stared up at the ceiling, Zach explored another possibility—one that only weeks before he would have considered forever out of the question.

Perhaps he could live in peace with his father after all these years!

Thirteen

KID BUNNING WAS IN town alone.

It was past noon; but the sun, burning down out of a cloudless sky, sent its rays bouncing with cruel intensity off the hard-packed street up into the Kid's gray eyes. Though it did little good, the Kid kept the brim of his black, flatcrowned hat down over his eyes.

As the Kid strode along the wooden sidewalk, giving not an inch to any in his path, he was fully aware of the active dislike his presence stirred in the townspeople. Women averted their eyes. Children ducked down alleys, then watched curiously as he passed. Small groups grew suddenly silent until he had gone by. He was like a shark swimming in unfriendly waters. At times like this, the Kid told himself, he did not want—or need—others to like him. All he wanted was their respect. If they would not grant him that, then he would accept their fear instead. No one messed with someone they feared. It was the only security the Kid had ever known.

The Belle Fourche loomed just across the street. The sound of its tinkling piano reminded the Kid of his enormous thirst. He crossed the street, strode up onto the sidewalk, and shouldered in through the saloon's batwings.

After the street's shimmering glare, the sudden darkness of the saloon momentarily blinded him. He paused for a moment. The sound of the doors swinging back and forth spread an ominous warning throughout the instantly silent room. The Kid started for the bar.

When he reached the bar, his vision returning, he found himself staring into the twin bores of a sawed-off shotgun. The barkeep who held it wore an eyepatch. He was vaguely familiar to the Kid. And then he remembered. This was the same fellow he and Nate had worked over the last time they had visited this place. Hell! He had heard that this jasper had left town, along with the clerk in the land office.

Only he hadn't, it seemed.

"Put that cannon away," the Kid said quietly. "I didn't come in here to make trouble. All I want is a drink. There ain't no law against that."

"Yes, there is. For you there is. At least in this saloon."

The Kid spun. "Who says so?"

Jane Durrell was walking toward him. "I do!" she said.

The woman was carrying a shotgun also. It was a brand new Greener, its twin barrels gleaming dully.

For just a moment the Kid considered turning and leaving. But only for a moment. He had entered this whore's place for a drink. There was no law against that. He would be damned if he would show his heels to this woman.

He couldn't afford to do such a thing.

"Put that shotgun down, whore," the Kid said softly, contemptuously, "before I ram it up your—"

Jane let go both barrels. The hellish reverberation wiped out the rest of the Kid's sentence. She did not fire the shotgun at him, just over his head. Nevertheless, burning bits of powder struck him in the face. The blast deafened him, rocked him back. His knees turned to water. He took two uncertain steps backward.

The barkeep, his shotgun still trained on the Kid, smiled. "Just say one more word about Miss Durrell, you son of a bitch," the barkeep said softly, "and I'll blow your goddam head off."

"That'd be murder!" the Kid protested weakly.

"You think a jury in this town would convict me of murder if I blasted you? Hell, yo little turd, they'd give me a medal!"

The Kid felt the palms of his hands sweating. The hair on the back of his neck was standing up. Glancing quickly around him at the crowd, he saw that every face in the room was turned to him. And in each face he saw only hate—and in some a pure, naked lust to see him dead.

Suddenly the Kid wanted to run, but his feet seemed rooted to the saloon's floor.

"Go on!" Jane Durrell said. "Get out of here! Don't you or any Slash D rider show your face in here again! Now, git, polecat!"

Pulling himself together, the Kid straightened, turned around calmly, and, without a backward glance, strode easily from the place. It cost him dearly. Every step was a terror for him. He kept waiting for a blast of buckshot to punch a gaping hole in his back.

And then he was standing in the dazzling brightness of the street, a curious crowd watching him. They had been drawn by the single shotgun blast. The Kid took a deep breath. He was alive. His courage returned, like a whipped dog returning to its master.

He pushed his way boldly through the crowd, crossed the street and gained the sidewalk on the other side. He needed a drink, badly. The Long Spur was just ahead. He started for it, his step becoming more solid with each passing second.

But he was stung. He had been made to turn tail. His reputation was at stake. He would be finished in this valley as soon as word of what happened to him in the Belle Fourche got out. Somehow, soon, he had to recover the ground he had lost to that whore.

At that moment the devil answered his prayer.

Bill Handler was still slightly amused at the idea. Tobe Winston had stopped at the Flying T on his way into Canyon City to get supplies for Stirrup. When Tobe had admitted to Zach that he wasn't taking any Stirrup riders along for protection, Zach had suggested that Bill go along. He had a list of items his foreman needed to pick up in town. At the same time, Zach pointed out, Bill could act as Tobe's shotgun rider.

Thinking back on it, Bill had to laugh. Tobe was insulted to think Zach would think he needed a bodyguard. Less than a mile from the Flying T, he had fallen asleep, leaving the chore of driving the team to Bill. Now Tobe was inside the general store, dickering with the owner over the price of a keg of nails that Bill knew the old fourflusher had no intention whatsoever of buying.

Next time, Bill said to himself as he shouldered the last sack of flour and stepped off the porch, he would send Zach in to look after Tobe. Tipping his shoulder forward, Bill let the sack land as gently as possible on top of the four other sacks. A small puff of flour exploded from under the sack when it hit. Bill stepped back and brushed the palms of his hands against his pants' legs. Then he turned to wait for Tobe to emerge from the store.

Bill frowned.

The Kid was standing on the sidewalk between Bill and the store's entrance. The pale gunman was rocking slightly on his heels, watching Bill the way a coyote watches a rabbit hole. Bill felt a chill run up his spine. The Kid was on the prod—dangerously so. Something—Bill had no idea what—had primed him.

Just then Tobe hurried out of the store. Bill saw the old man glance quickly away from the near-blinding glare of the sun, then blunder clumsily into the Kid, jostling him slightly from the rear.

The Kid flung himself around. When he saw it was Tobe, he backhanded him with such sudden fury that he sent Tobe stumbling backward. Tobe's right shoulder struck a post, causing Tobe to spin and fall face down on the boardwalk. Tobe shook his head, dazed, then turned and looked up at the Kid.

"You didn't need to do that, you son of a bitch," Tobe said.

Instantly, the Kid's bright Smith & Wesson materialized in his right hand. He crouched, lips parted, eyes narrowing. He was like a stick of dynamite with only an inch of sputtering fuse left to go.

"Hold it, Kid," Bill cried.

The Kid spun to face him. "Stay out of this! That old bastard ain't goin' to call me no son of a bitch!"

A crowd had gathered on the instant. It was a silent, eager crowd. The smell of violence was in the air.

"Put that gun away and let's talk sensible," Bill said, aware that the Kid was no longer rational. "It was just an accident. Tobe didn't mean to bump into you. He was blinded by the sun and didn't see you."

"He deliberately ran into me!" the Kid cried, nursing his rage.

Tobe lurched angrily to his feet and started toward the Kid to protest. The Kid turned as Tobe neared him and cracked him across the side of the head with the barrel of his six-gun. When somehow Tobe managed to stay on his feet, the Kid followed after him, intent on repeating the punishment.

Bill clawed his six-gun from its holster. "Kid!" he cried. "Leave him be!"

The Kid glanced at Bill and saw the drawn gun in his hand. A sudden, maniacal light gleamed in his eyes. He swung about and fired.

Bill knew he should return the fire, but it was all happening so quickly. He felt the round pound into his gut, just above his navel. It felt as if someone had punched him. His breath gone, he was aware of himself stumbling backward. And then he was on his knees. He glanced back toward the Kid. Surprisingly, there was no pain. All he felt was astonishment.

He watched numbly as the Kid raised his revolver coolly and fired a second time, and a third—

* * *

Zach wanted to sit down. But he was standing on the narrow porch and there was no chair. Instead, he reached out for the porch post and grabbed it. He saw Tobe look away from his stricken face.

Zach heard himself say, for the second time: "Bill's *dead?*"

"It was the Kid, Zach. He was like a madman. He shot Bill three times!"

Zach turned around and started into the ranchhouse. "Come in, Tobe," he told the man. "Come inside and—rest up. You don't look so good."

Tobe climbed down from the wagon, tied the reins around the brake lever, and followed Zach inside the house. Zach waited for him, then led the way into the kitchen. Realizing there was no coffee, Zach started to wash out the coffee pot, then suddenly gave it up and sat down at the kitchen table.

Tobe sat down across from him. "Your face, Tobe," Zach said. "Was that the Kid's doing, too?"

Tobe nodded grimly.

"Let's have it, then. I want to know what happened."

Tobe plunged into his account, emphasizing at the end of it that he was still at a loss to understand the blind rage that seemed to have governed the Kid.

"The Kid was after you, and then he turned on Bill. That it?" Zach asked, trying, like Tobe, to make some sense out of it.

"That's right. He seemed wild. I just bumped into him and he exploded. He would have killed me, Zach. Bill saved my life." Tobe reached his hand up to feel of the ugly welt that had blossomed on his left cheekbone. He was, Zach realized, as stricken as Zach was. Tobe shook his head. "It was all my fault. I should've watched where I was going. But the sun was so bright, coming out of that store—" His voice trailed off.

"Don't think about that, Tobe. You can't blame

yourself when you get bitten by a mad dog. The only thing you can do is find the mad dog—and kill it."

Tobe nodded dully. "Yeah. I guess you're right, Zach."

"You want me to ride back with you, Tobe?"

"No. That's all right, Zach. Just get me one of your hands to help unload your stuff, would you? I'm plumb wore out."

"Sure, Tobe," Zach said. "You wait right here and I'll see to it."

Zach got up and walked past Tobe to the door, resting his hand lightly on the old man's shoulder as he passed him.

The moon's wash turned the lush pastures to silver and the Little Whiskey into a bottomless ribbon of black satin. As they splashed across it, their horses forced to strain against the still-swift waters, the three riders said not a word. Zach was in the lead. Behind him were LeBeau and Manny Garcia. These two, like Zach, had ridden with Bill since first he had signed on as a cowpuncher in Texas.

Zach hadn't had to ask them to go with him. It had been their idea from the start.

As they left the river behind, the moon's bright eye sank behind the mountains. It would be light soon, Zach realized. They had ridden through the night and would most likely reach the Slash D a little after sunup.

Soon enough.

Zach thought about Bill. He had sent Thompson in to Canyon City to tend to the details concerning Bill's burial. Zach had explained to Thompson that he wanted his foreman to be buried in the same graveyard as his mother, as close to her grave as they could get it. He had explained that he would like to hold off on the funeral until he could get there, which he hoped would be the next day.

But Zach did not want to attend Bill's funeral. Not really. He did not want to have to listen to those clumps of earth falling on his friend's coffin. For Zach it was as if a needed weight had been removed suddenly from the scales—and now everything was out of kilter; nothing seemed right, somehow. When Tobe left, Zach had tried to imagine Bill's face: his laughing eyes, especially, since it was the man's humor—no matter what the conditions were—that had made him such a good companion on the trail. But he had been unable to fix Bill's image in his mind. And then it was that he realized how complete was his loss. The memory of a man was no substitute for his living presence.

He had sent Bill in with Tobe; he should have gone in with Tobe himself.

That thought stung him and continued to burrow, like a fishhook, into his conscience. The only consolation he would allow himself was the knowledge that this time he was going himself.

The first warm rays of the morning sun were branding the compound's hard-packed ground when Dudley, finished with breakfast and having given his men the day's assignments, strode across the compound to the horse stable. Silas had been unusually silent during breakfast; short with him, in fact. And Dudley was getting sick of it. Maybe it was time for the old wrangler to pack his bedroll and drift.

"Silas!" he called into the barn.

Fresh manure was steaming in the gutters back of the stalls; the polished, chestnut flanks of the show and harness stock gleamed dully in the dim light. Bright green bottle flies buzzed. Tails swished. Heavy, restless forefeet thudded dully, like distant thunder.

"Silas!" Dudley called a second time, louder. He stepped into the barn and picked his way carefully around the moist, trampled hay and the fresh horse manure. The smell was pungent; Dudley found it bracing. It was a good clean, familiar smell, that of strong, well-cared-for horses. Like most cattlemen, he had grown up with it.

Silas appeared from behind an empty stall. He was

blinking tears hastily from his eyes; there was a hip flask in his hand. The man had obviously been drinking his fuel for the day's activity. He screwed the top of the flask back on, then dropped the flask into his hip pocket and grabbed a pitchfork.

"What the hell you doin' in here, Dudley?" the old man wanted to know. "You takin' to visitin' the lowlife, have you?"

"Goddamn it, Silas. This is my stable. And you're working for me. When the hell are you going to start remembering that?"

"I see. You come in here to pull rank on me." Silas poked the pitchfork into a neat pile of hay inside the empty stall, lifted a sizable portion, then, staggering only slightly, deftly fed the hay into the nearest stall. The horse in the stall seemed to appreciate the attention and nodded its head vigorously up and down.

"That's not why I came in here, damn it. I came in here because you've been getting pretty difficult to deal with lately, and I'm getting sick of it."

Silas straightened, then leaned forward on the pitchfork's handle and fixed Dudley with a cold eye. "How sick?"

Dudley could not respond at once. He looked away from his wrangler's cold eyes. As usual, he found himself on the defensive whenever he approached the man. Well, damn it, not this time. He looked back at Silas. "Sick enough to tell you to get your time or quit acting like you're the one who owns this spread. And I want you to cut down on your boozing."

"You don't want much, and that's a fact."

"What's the matter with you, Silas? You don't seem to appreciate nothing I've done for you. And you don't care about anything."

"Do *you* care about anything, Dudley?"

"Now what the hell is that supposed to mean?"

"Do you care what your pet mad dog did yesterday in Canyon City?"

"The Kid? He shot Handler in self-defense. Half the town witnessed it. You heard Pike. You heard what he said when he rode in with the Kid. It's easy to see what happened. Zach's foreman thought that just because I've let them alone that me and my men were no longer going to stand up to them range grabbers." Dudley took a deep breath. "I'm glad the Kid stood up to Handler."

As if on cue, the saddle horse in the stall beside Dudley began to void a thick steaming gout of urine. Dudley looked down and saw that his Levi's were being spattered as the heavy yellow stream pounded into the steaming mash of manure and straw about the horse's fetlocks. Dudley moved hastily to one side. Silas laughed.

"Seems like that animal knows horse shit when he hears it," the wrangler drawled.

Dudley was suddenly furious. This time Silas had really gone too far. "Damn you! What the hell do you mean by that? What the Kid did was right. No Slash D rider's goin' to stand still for being made a fool of! Not while I'm around he ain't."

"You mean not while that killer's around."

"I think maybe you're getting too old for this job, Silas," Dudley said coldly. "The way I see it, you've overstayed your welcome."

"That's the way I see it, too, Dudley," Silas said, his voice surprisingly strong. "I don't want to be here when your son comes by looking for the Kid. I might find myself on Zach's side."

"Isn't that where you've been all along?"

"Maybe so. Maybe from the moment I saw what you did to that man's Ma."

"Get out, Silas! I'll have what wages are due you waiting in my office. I want you off this compound before noon!"

Dudley spun on his heels and stalked out of the barn. He was so furious when he hit the bright sunlight of the compound that he didn't hear one of his men was calling to him as, head down, he strode angrily through the glare toward the ranch office. It was the sound of running footsteps that caused him to look up.

One of his hands was approaching, excitement in his eyes. Dudley pulled up impatiently. "Well, what is it?"

"Some riders are coming, Mr. Stuart."

"Riders?" Dudley turned quickly around, squinting in the low, early-morning sun. "Where?"

But he didn't need the cowhand's help any longer. He saw the riders clearly. Three of them. They were passing through the cottonwood grove in the near flat. Even at this distance, Dudley recognized the tall, erect figure of his son riding in the lead. Dudley thought then of Silas's words just a moment before and groaned inwardly.

Dudley swung back to the cowhand. "Where's the Kid?"

"Inside the bunkhouse." The fellow grinned slightly, careful not to show any disrespect to the boss. "Cleanin' his gun, most likely."

"Tell him to stay out of sight and keep out of sight. Tell him I'll have his hide if he shows himself!"

The hand looked at Dudley in surprise. It was not a command he had expected.

"Do it, damn you! Now!"

The cowhand turned and hurried across the compound, heading for the cookshack. Dudley looked back at the three riders. They were making no effort to hide their presence. If their mission was what Dudley assumed it was, they were being incredibly foolhardy. And courageous, as well. For a moment he felt a dim flickering of pride that the man in the lead was his son.

As he rode into the Slash D compound, Zach's gaze flicked about quickly. There were at least eight Slash D hands watching him from various vantage points, some standing in front of the stable, others by the blacksmith shop, three in front of the cookshack. He saw the aproned cook standing in front of his kitchen door, an enormous shotgun in his hand.

Again Zach noted the weathered ruin of a two-story frame house, the construction of which seemed to have been halted arbitrarily—on a moment's notice, it seemed. A pitiful reminder of broken dreams, it was hidden, like something shameful, in among the cottonwoods. He had since learned from Jane that this was the palatial mansion Dudley had been in the act of building for himself, his wife, and his unborn son. According to Jane, on the day following his abandonment of his wife before Miss Helen's place, he had driven the carpenters and masons from the site like a madman, firing over their heads as they drove frantically off in their wagons.

Zach looked straight ahead of him now—at the small group of men awaiting him in front of the ranchhouse. Dudley was standing on the narrow porch. In front of the porch, serving as a rough picket line, were four of Slash D's toughest riders. Nate Claw was standing directly in front of Dudley.

Zach frowned. Where was the Kid?

He kept riding until he was within ten yards of the porch, then pulled up. Garcia pulled to a halt on his left, LeBeau on his right. There was a reasonable distance between them. It had been decided earlier that they did not want to make too easy a target by bunching.

"Where's the Kid, Dudley?" Zach asked, patting the coiled bullwhip he had hung over his pommel. "I want him."

"You're not the law, Zach. And you're trespassing on Slash D land."

"The law's in your back pocket. We all know that. So it looks like we'll just have to make our own law in this valley. That's why I want the Kid."

Dudley frowned. "You got some idea you can bring him in to Canyon City and lock him up, even though you ain't the law?"

Zach paused a moment before answering. "Nope," he said quietly. "That wasn't what I had in mind at all."

"I thought not. Well, he's under my protection. And

he'll stay under my protection. He's a Slash D rider, and that's good enough for me."

"He's a Slash D killer!"

"That isn't the way I heard it. Sheriff Pike's got witnesses. Your man provoked the Kid. The Kid fired in self-defense."

"Three times! He fired three times in self-defense! He was provoked because old Tobe Winston blundered into him? Do you really intend to shield that man from justice, Dudley?"

"I buried two of my men not long ago because of you, Zach. I don't intend to let you get your hands on another one of my men. Now I suggest you turn around and ride on out of here. I've told my men not to fire on you. And they won't—no matter what fool thing you might do. But I remind you. You are trespassing on Slash D land. I have already saved your life, Zach. Someday you'll thank me."

"I want the Kid. I want your hired gun out here."

Nate stepped forward and took the bridle of Zach's horse in his right hand. Glancing up at Zach, he smiled thinly. "You heard what your father said, Zach. Ride out of here. Now!" Then he started to pull Zach's horse around.

You heard what your father said!

Those words rang in Zach's head like a mind-numbing scream. Instantly, Zach drew his six-gun and brought it down on Nate's head. The sound of the barrel glancing off the foreman's skull carried to every man in that tight circle. Knocked senseless, Nate let go of Zach's horse and sprawled backward on the ground.

Then, holstering his six-gun, Zach uncoiled his bullwhip so swiftly that it was almost a kind of sorcery as the long lash snaked out like something alive and snapped cruelly around his father's shoulder and neck. As soon as the lash dug in, Zach flung his horse around and yanked Dudley off the porch.

Ignoring his father's startled cry, Zach galloped back across the compound, LeBeau and Garcia keeping pace with him. His father, barely conscious, was dragged along after him. Zach was almost out of the ranch's compound before the whip released Dudley.

Zach reined in, spun his horse about, and snaked his whip out a second time. Dudley had been in the act of struggling to his feet, a crimson slash across his cheek, when Zach's whip snapped about his shoulders. With a sudden roar of outrage and pain, Dudley grabbed hold of the braided rawhide and tried to pull the whip from Zach's grasp. Zach simply yanked the whip cruelly, pulling Dudley off his feet. The man sprawled face forward into the dust. The whip fell loose and Zach snapped it back and brought it down again on his father's back. This time the tip cut a piece of flesh from his neck. The man cried out in pain, scrambled to his feet, and turned to run.

Zach caught him from behind, the whip coiling about his legs. The man fell. Then he rolled over and clawed frantically at the rawhide still wrapped around his legs. Expertly, Zach flicked the whip, releasing his father's legs, then with a series of snapping strokes reduced his father's white cotton shirt to bloody tatters. Rolling over onto his stomach, his shoulders hunched to protect his head, Dudley began to crawl away as Zach continued to whip him with a deft, controlled series of strokes that snapped like gunshots. Almost instantly, Dudley's back was transformed into a raw, ribboned slab of beefsteak.

By this time, Dudley's cowhands—having raced on foot across the compound with drawn guns—were pulling to a halt just behind Dudley. Nate, his senses recovered, was in the lead.

"Stop it!" Nate cried, dropping to one knee beside Dudley. "That's enough! You'll kill him!"

Zach pulled in his whip, coiled it, then hung it over his saddle horn. He kept his eyes on Dudley as the man sat up slowly, then turned his head to stare dazedly up at Zach. The old rancher's face was a network of raw slashes.

"How did that feel, Dudley?" Zach asked.

Dudley gasped something and struggled to his feet, swaying like a dazed steer that has just run into a fence post. His hand went up to his cheek and came away bloody. Blinking in dismay, he looked back up at Zach.

Leaning forward over the pommel, Zach looked coldly down at his father. "Now, you know what my mother felt that night you dragged her across this compound and beat her into a cripple."

With a fierce bellow of rage, Dudley snatched from Nate the gun his foreman was holding. He brought it up quickly. The sound of it being cocked came clearly in the hushed silence. The old rancher's hand was steady, his face resolute, his eyes burning now with a maniacal intensity.

Zach knew he could not outdraw his father. But that didn't matter any longer. He felt a wild recklessness, an eagerness to finish this business once and for all right here.

"No!" one of Dudley's men cried. Bursting from the awed crowd of punchers, he knocked Dudley's six-gun aside. It was the old wrangler who had come for the Slash D horses. "I ain't gonna let you!" the old man cried. "I ain't gonna stand by and watch this time!"

Furious, Dudley turned on the wrangler and clubbed him repeatedly about the face and head, driving him into the ground. Blood gouted from one of the old man's nostrils. He twisted away from Dudley, groaning—as Dudley turned his six-gun once again on Zach.

But Zach had taken up his whip a second time. It snaked out, biting into Dudley's wrist and holding fast. The six-gun fell to the ground. Zach whirled his horse about and galloped from the compound, again dragging Dudley along behind him. At last, as the whip released the rancher, shots exploded from the ranks of the outraged punchers.

A round whistled just over Zach's head. He glanced back. Dudley was struggling to get up onto his feet, his men swarming past him on foot, still firing at Zach. Zach turned about in his saddle and bent low—just in time to feel a bullet sledge into his left shoulder, slamming him still further over his pommel. Zach's sudden shift of weight threw his mount momentarily off-stride. The horse stumbled, but managed to stay upright—and keep going.

"You going to be all right, Zach?" LeBeau called, guiding his mount closer to Zach's.

Zach nodded. "Sure," he managed grimly. "Only you two better stay close. If I fall off, I'll want you to catch me, then tie me back on."

There were no more shots from behind them. They crested a slight ridge, then dipped into the sweeping meadow beyond. Ahead of Zach stretched a long ride, and he wasn't sure he was going to make it. The numbness had given away to a hot and searing throb that radiated throughout his whole shoulder. He felt a gray sense of futility.

He was fleeing, severely wounded, from the Slash D—and the Kid remained under Dudley Stuart's protection, well beyond the reach of justice.

Fourteen

THE STREETS OF CANYON City were silent, the only light the almost negligible glow that came from the dim orange peel of a moon that hung low in the sky. It was well past midnight. The saloons had long since closed. A single cowboy, the back of his jacket matted with wet hay, his hat crooked, staggered from the livery stable. He walked down the center of the deserted street and climbed the sidewalk and disappeared into The Drover's Hotel, a narrow, unpainted wood structure beside The Long Spur. The stillness of the town had been barely broken by the cowboy's progress. With his disappearance inside, the town's deathly stillness reasserted itself. The orange sliver of a moon had dropped closer to the horizon. Canyon City slept in silence under a deepening blanket of darkness.

Abruptly, the sleep of the town was shattered by the thunder of many hooves. The sound came from the northwest and grew rapidly in volume. Riders exploded onto Main Street, raced along its hard-packed surface, then pulled up in front of the darkened Belle Fourche.

Kid Bunning was in the lead, his horse sliding to a hock-rattling stop at the saloon's tie rail. The Kid was off his mount in an instant. The riders behind him followed, mounting the boardwalk in front of the saloon. All of them carried unlit lanterns. The eight men huddled together for a moment as the Kid lit each lantern.

With all eight lanterns glowing, the Kid spoke to two of his most burly men. The two rushed the locked doors of the saloon. Their combined bulk crashed through into the Belle Fourche, with the Kid and the others on their heels. The sound of their boots in the deserted saloon filled the night; then came the sound of shattering glass.

Out of the saloon the men poured. They mounted swiftly and watched for a moment as the inside of the saloon began to glow like the interior of a pot-bellied stove. The Kid was the last to leave. He turned in the doorway and flung his lantern. The sound of it exploding was lost in the larger sound of the flames roaring at the walls and licking at the ceiling. Tongues of fire were already beating against the windows.

The Kid mounted and emptied his revolver at the windows. With the sudden rush of air, the flames exploded with a mighty *whoosh!* The sudden, searing heat drove the riders back momentarily. The Kid yanked his horse around and led the riders back down Main Street. They were gone as swiftly as they had come, leaving the Belle Fourche and the rooms above it a searing, thunderous torch leaping skyward, filling the no longer empty streets with a ruddy, hellish glow. Above the cries of the citizens trying to organize a bucket brigade could be heard the terrified, soul-wrenching screams of the women trapped inside the building.

Even as the Kid's forces approached Canyon City, Dudley Stuart led a storm of riders into the Diamond Cross compound. They, too, carried lanterns; they lit them in front of the darkened ranchhouse and bunkhouse, then spread out to send them arcing through the night, some to crash through bunkhouse windows, others to land with a blazing explosion upon roofs, and still others rolling into the entrance of barns and stables. Dudley himself, a guttering lantern held in his right hand, galloped toward the L-shaped ranchhouse. Pulling up in front of it, he saw a stunned Dave Snyder—his wife crowding out of the door beside him—standing in the open doorway in a bathrobe, a shotgun in his hand.

Behind Dudley a growing brightness materialized. The night's silence was punctured by the sporadic firing of Dudley's men as they began sending rounds through the bunkhouse's windows. In the raw light Dudley saw the disbelief on Mary Snyder's face, the fear mingled with fury on Snyder's.

"Dudley!" Mary cried, dashing off the porch toward him. "Dudley! You promised me! You promised!"

Dudley swore. "Get back, woman! That was your idea, not mine!"

But by that time she had hold of his bridle, and was reaching up to grab the lantern in his hand. Dudley dropped his reins and with his left hand back-handed her, sending her reeling to the ground. Then he snatched up his reins, charged closer to the house and flung the lantern up onto the roof. It exploded, sending a shower of sparks down across the porch roof and a sudden, darting flame across the shingles.

Snyder bolted furiously out of the doorway and raised his shotgun as Dudley galloped past. Dudley cut sharply on his reins. His horse almost foundered, it turned so quickly. A grin on his raw, striped face, Dudley pulled out his own oversized Colt and fired. He caught the man low—as he intended—smashing one leg out from under him. As Snyder crumpled, the shotgun fired, sending its load of buckshot whistling over Dudley's head.

Four other riders galloped over to join Dudley, the remaining lanterns swinging like malevolent fireflies in their hands, and he swung his horse around to meet them. Too late, he saw Mary Snyder—on her feet, her arms waving frantically—stumble blindly into his horse's path. The horse shied away as Dudley swore and sawed back on his reins.

She was calling out to him, reminding him of his

promise to her, when the lunging horse struck her. The horse reared, almost unseating Dudley—and when its front hooves came down, Dudley knew at once that one of them had not come down on solid ground.

Dudley dismounted from the still shying horse and found Mary lying in a pool of her own blood, her neck a shattered piece of flowing darkness, her head lying at such an odd angle that it was instantly clear to Dudley that her neck was broken.

Riders surrounded them. Dudley looked up at the nearest one.

"Throw your slicker over her. I don't have mine with me."

As the man dismounted and pulled his yellow slicker from his bedroll, Dudley looked around at the burning roof of the ranchhouse. Snyder was crawling toward them, one hand clutching his shatterd thigh, the flames from the roof behind him highlighting his drawn, distraught features.

Dudley strode toward him. "She's dead, Snyder," Dudley said brutally.

"Why, Stuart? What did she mean?"

"It wasn't my idea, Snyder. She came to me of her own free will. She thought I'd listen to her. For a while I did. I'm sorry about this. But it doesn't change anything. Get out as soon as you can ride. You're finished here."

"You can't leave us like this!"

"I can and will," Dudley said, turning back to his horse.

"Dudley!" the prostrate man cried. "You'll pay for this! That son of yours will see to it, if I don't."

Dudley spun to look back at Snyder. "It's that son of mine you've got to thank for this, Snyder. Your wife understood that. Too bad you didn't."

He mounted up and trotted over to join his riders who had been waiting for him in a semicircle around the dead woman. To the few riders still carrying lanterns, he nodded curtly. They spurred their horses past the downed

Snyder and flung their lanterns through the ranchhouse windows and up onto the roof.

By this time a ragged line of Diamond Cross cowhands were moving across the compound toward them. Their fire was getting hot, and they kept on relentlessly, despite the return fire of Dudley's men. When Dudley saw one of his riders drop his six-gun and clutch at his arm, he waved his men back, and galloping to their head, led them from the blazing compound.

Tobe Winston had been a light sleeper ever since a herd he was trailing north in '71 stampeded, knocking the chuck wagon over onto him. It had left him with a few broken bones and a permanant inability to sleep soundly when trouble was possible. As a result Tobe was out of his bunk the moment the first faint sound of thundering hooves came to him. When Nate Claw led his band of Slash D riders into Stirrup's ranch, Tobe and Sullivan were at the windows of their ranchhouse, and the rest of Stirrup's cowhands were positioned at strategic locations about the compound.

Tobe's first shot winged one of the Slash D marauders. From that moment on, the firing from both sides was intense. But the night was dark with only the faint orange sliver of a moon for light, and soon the air was dark filled with arcing lanterns. The stables went first, the bunkhouse and the cookshack next. Then the ranchhouse became the focus of their attention. It cost the riders—more than three marauders peeled away, their lanterns crashing to the ground—but Nate's men were persistent, and soon Tobe and Sullivan could hear the roaring of the flames from the roof. As the smoke seeped down through the rafters, obscuring their vision and searing their lungs, other lanterns crashed through their windows. After that, Sullivan and Tobe were firing blindly into the night from the bowels of a roaring inferno.

With every structure in flames, Nate's riders charged out of Stirrup's compound and disappeared into the night. Sullivan and Tobe staggered from the flaming ranchhouse, then raced across the compound toward the horse barns. The sound of the squealing, terrified animals sent shudders through each of the men. Two of the Stirrup's men disappeared into the nearest barn before Sullivan and Tobe reached it. A moment later the men led four wild-eyed horses out of the flaming building. But when Sullivan and Tobe started into the barn after the other horses, they were driven back by the searing heat . . .

The storm of hooves clattering up to the door of her ranchhouse awakened Sue Torgeson. She was slipping into a bathrobe when the pounding on her door began. It infuriated her, and it was this anger that carried her through the next few minutes as she lit a lantern, carried it through the dark house, and pulled open the door.

A nervous cowhand she didn't recognize was standing on the porch. Behind him were four horsemen, all strangers. They kept the brims of their hats well down over their eyes. To Sue, they looked like overgrown schoolboys who had been caught playing hooky.

The man standing on the porch swallowed nervously. He did not remove his hat, and Sue could tell he was bracing himself not to be intimidated by the fact that she was a woman.

"What is it?" she demanded of him. "Why are you pounding on my door at this hour?"

As she said this, she glanced past the man at her bunkhouse. She was pleased to see that lights were appearing behind the windows. These riders had awakened her men, and she felt encouraged. Much of her fear abated, and she found herself thinking that these men were undoubtedly from the same pack that had killed her father. Realizing this, she felt only anger as she stared at the cowhand.

"Ma'am," the fellow said, "I been told to ride here and tell you to get out of this here valley."

Sue straightened, thrusting her shoulders back angrily. "Have you? I see. Not content with killing my father, you've come for me. Is that it, mister?"

"No damn it, ma'am, that ain't it. Not exactly. Dudley Stuart just told me to tell you to get out of this valley because the rest of your stock is gone now, and your fencin' is down, as well." The fellow moistened his lips. "You ain't got no more reason for stayin' in this valley—or for helping Zach Stuart."

"Is that all, mister?"

"Yes, ma'am. That's what I was sent to tell you."

"Well, you did fine, mister. You delivered your message. Now you go back to that old bastard and deliver *my* message. You tell him that I been thinking maybe I shouldn't side with Zach in his vendetta against your boss. That's what I was considering. But not now. You tell Dudley Stuart I'm going to do everything I can to help Zach stop him. Did you hear me, mister?"

Cowed by her anger, the cowhand nodded. "Yes, ma'am, I heard you."

"Now get off this ranch!"

He stepped quickly back off the porch and mounted up. By that time Sue's cowhands were out of the bunkhouse and were trotting across the compound toward her. Some of her men were carrying revolvers. Raising her lantern still higher to throw more light on the five horsemen, she stepped out onto the porch.

Dudley Stuart's men dragged their mounts around swiftly and galloped from the compound. Sue lowered her lantern and watched them ride off, tears streaming down her cheeks. She was furious with herself for crying; but Dudley Stuart's arrogance in sending those riders only served to remind her once again of the senseless brutality that had taken her father from her.

* * *

When Sue rode into the Flying T ranch that same morning, it was close to ten o'clock. She had been riding since Dudley Stuart's men left her place, without stopping to rest. Her mount's flanks were streaked with lather as she reined up in front of Zach's ranchhouse. A few of Zach's hands were watching from the stables and the bunkhouse, as Cookie rushed out of the ranchhouse to take her horse.

"Hello, Cookie," Sue said, dismounting wearily. "How's Zach?"

"He ain't so good, Miss Sue. I washed out that shoulder wound of his with some awful good fresh whiskey, but he's still got the fever."

"Did you get the bullet out?"

"Oh, I got that out, all right," Cookie said proudly. "And Zach was so drunk he only yelped a few times. But like I said, he's got the fever—so I figure the wound got infected."

Sue smiled wearily at Cookie. "I haven't been much help, Cookie, have I."

"That's all right, Miss Sue. You got problems of your own, I reckon."

Sue rested her hand lightly on Cookie's arm. "Yes, I do have problems of my own. But that should not have prevented me from coming when I heard about Zach's wound. Is he up yet?"

"No, he ain't. He's asleep, still. I wanted him to get all the sleep he could. Most of the time he's just been tossin' about and wishin' he could get up."

"I won't wake him. I'll just wait for him to wake up." She smiled then and looked pleadingly at Cookie. "I'm afraid I haven't had any breakfast. Would you mind if I went in there and used your kitchen?"

"You go right in where Zach is. Pull up a chair and rest. I'll call you when breakfast is ready." He smiled, his long face suddenly transformed. "I got some fresh doughnut batter."

Sue thanked Cookie and walked inside to Zach's bedroom and slumped wearily down into a wooden chair at the foot of Zach's bed. Zach was breathing shallowly. His face was flushed, but he was lying quietly. His shoulder was hidden by bandages made from a torn shirt, and Sue noted with relief that they were not stained with blood.

She was astonished at how Zach's illness had transformed him into a younger twin of his father. There was a dark stubble on his chin, his cheeks were sunken, his closed eyes lost in deep hollows; all of this accentuated Zach's high, square forehead, the solid, dominating brows, and especially the long, haggard lines of his face. Had Zach worn a mustache like his father's, the resemblance would have been uncanny.

A faint alarm stirred within her. How could she expect this man to lead them against his own blood? And then it occurred to her that Zach was more than just his father done over; he was the fruit of his father and his mother's union. His mother's softness and gentleness lived within him, as well as his father's arrogance and capacity to hate. But which side of his nature, she wondered, would win his soul in the end? She sighed and settled back in her chair to wait for him to awaken.

Zach opened his eyes. It was almost noon. A broad beam of sunlight was streaming in the window. He stirred and found himself focusing his eyes on Sue Torgeson. She was sitting in a chair at the foot of the bed. He looked at her for a long moment, finding it difficult to believe his eyes. His fevered imagination of the past three days had at times populated this room of his with far more terrible apparitions.

"That you, Sue?" he asked, smiling.

She got up from the chair and walked over to stand beside him. "Yes," she said, looking down at him with concern in her eyes. "It's me. How do you feel?"

He let his head rest back on the pillow. "Much better. My fever's gone, I think. But I feel as weak as a kitten. Would you tell Cookie I'm hungry?"

"Yes, of course. I think that's good news," she said, turning to leave the room.

"No need to rush out," he protested. "You could just call Cookie."

"Don't worry," Sue said, slipping through the doorway. "I won't get lost."

Sue's presence galvanized Zach. As soon as she left his room, he got up and dressed. It was not as easy a task as he had imagined it to be, but he appeared in the kitchen just as Cookie was loading up the tray to take to him. Sue laughed at his groggy appearance and joined him at the kitchen table, sipping coffee.

It was good to be out of the bed, to be sitting up at a table. The conversation with Sue he kept light, even though he sensed that she was not here just for the visit. Zach wanted to enjoy this meal with Sue before facing up to whatever ugliness his father had brought about while he was on his back. He could not believe that his father would not want to strike back at them now. But the important thing for Zach at that moment was that Sue had come to the Flying T on her own accord, that she no longer seemed so opposed to his presence here in the valley.

"All right, Sue," Zach said, pulling his second mug of coffee toward him. "What is it? What's brought you here? What's my father up to now?"

"Your father sent riders to my place last night, Zach."

Zach frowned. "Riders?"

"There were five in all. One rider told me the rest of my stock was gone and so I had no more reason for staying in this valley—or for helping you."

Zach sat suddenly back in his chair, furious at his father's arrogance. "And what did you tell him, Sue?"

Her face colored. "Do you doubt what I told him? You

know how I feel about this valley. And besides, what kind of a response would my father have given?"

Zach smiled slightly. "I'm sorry, Sue. I didn't mean to imply anything when I asked that. I was pretty sure what kind of a response you'd send back to my father."

"Were you?"

He nodded. "But the important thing now is what you're going to do. You say the rest of your stock is gone?"

"That's what the cowboy said. I sent my foreman out to look see, then rode over here."

"Why?"

"To tell you, of course."

"There's more to it than that."

She looked suddenly down at the cup of coffee enfolded in her two hands. Zach glimpsed Cookie hastily wiping his hands on his apron and hurrying out the kitchen door. He was being discreet, Zach realized.

"It's hard for me to tell you," she said. "I'm so ashamed."

"You know who tipped off my father before I raided Indian Springs?"

She looked at him in astonishment, her face suddenly white. "How did you know that?"

He smiled. "I had a hunch."

"I should have told you before this. It was Mary Snyder. She thought—she thought Dudley was a lonely man—and that she could prevail upon him to spare the Diamond Cross."

"Prevail upon him?" Zach smiled slightly.

Sue blushed. "Mary is not as frumpy as she appears, Zach. And it is not her fault. Her husband never goes—near her. There's just nothing there."

"But you mean she's turned to Dudley?"

"In a strange way, she admires your father, Zach. I guess she finds his strength and decisiveness—no matter what its direction—a welcome contrast to Dave." She looked away from Zach's probing eyes. "Oh, I don't know how to explain it, Zach. But there it is. You're right. You can't trust members of the Association. Whatever move you plan, Mary will tell your father. And I just felt I had to warn you before our next meeting."

"Thank you, Sue. I appreciate your coming to me with this. What it means is any future action we take against Dudley, we will take without informing the Diamond Cross."

"You won't tell Dave, then."

Zach shook his head. "I'll let him find it out for himself. Maybe Mary will come to her senses, and he will never have to know."

At that moment hooves sounded in the compound. Zach turned his head and looked out the window. It was a rider, coming fast on a lathered horse. Zach recognized him as a Stirrup hand.

"We got more trouble, Sue," Zach said, moving to the kitchen doorway. "Looks like you weren't the only one to get a visit last night."

Sue moved to the kitchen doorway with Zach, her hand gripping his right arm to help support him. In his weakened state, Zach found he was grateful for Sue's help. The floor had tipped alarmingly under him when he got to his feet.

"Light and rest," Zach called as the weary rider pulled up to the tie rail and slumped momentarily forward over his pommel. "We got fresh coffee on."

"Much obliged," the rider said. "Ken Sullivan told me not to waste any time telling you. So I'll tell you now before I fall off this horse."

"Then out with it."

"The Diamond Cross's been burned out. Mary Snyder's dead and Dave's wounded bad. We've been burned out, too. Our stock's missing, the range's picked clean. You better check to see what you got left, Mr. Stuart."

"Light and rest," repeated Zach, glancing with sudden weariness at Sue and going back inside the ranchhouse.

It seemed he no longer had to worry about Mary. She

wasn't a problem any more. And that was good, he supposed, because there were a whole hell of a lot of other problems coming his way.

His father had let his dogs loose at last—and it looked as if he was not holding any of them back.

Fifteen

IT WAS A WEEK later. Two days before, Zach had ridden in to Canyon City to attend the funeral for Jane and four of her girls. The long ride had weakened Zach so much that Sue had insisted he spend yesterday in bed. Now he was moving restlessly about the living room, his second cup of coffee in his hand. The silence of the morning was broken suddenly by the sound of running footsteps. Putting down his coffee, Zach opened the door and saw LeBeau hurriedly mounting the porch steps.

"What's the matter?" Zach asked.

"You got a visitor."

Zach followed Pierre's gaze and saw one of his riders trailing a dim figure stumbling on foot toward the ranch. Since Zach intended to be ready for his father's next move, he had stationed this rider and others at strategic posts surrounding the ranch. Curious, Zach looked closely at the man his rider was herding toward them. The distance was too great for Zach to make out the fellow's features; but there was something vaguely familiar about him.

"Tell that rider to get back to his post, Pierre," Zach said, "I'm going inside for my hat. I'll be right out."

As LeBeau left the porch, Zach turned and went into the ranchhouse. He was a little shaky on his feet and had to reach out for the corner of a table as he hurried through the kitchen to his room. He still had to be careful about getting up or moving about too quickly, but he had been on his feet most of the morning and was actually feeling stronger with each passing hour. Sue had gone back to the Running H to see what she could do to put heart back into those of her riders who still remained. Zach missed her.

He found his hat, pulled it down snugly, slipped into his vest, and strapped his gunbelt around his waist. Then he strode out of the house as boldly as he could manage, hurrying to overtake LeBeau. He reached his new foreman as the man was calling to the rider, sending him back to his lookout post. By that time Zach recognized the fellow stumbling through the midmorning glare toward them. It was the Slash D wrangler who had saved Zach's life by pushing aside Dudley Stuart's six-gun.

"Come on," Zach said urgently. "Let's go help that old duffer. He might have walked all the way from Slash D!"

As soon as the wrangler saw Zach and Pierre hurrying toward him, he pulled himself to a halt. He swayed slightly in his tracks. He was without a hat. A bloody bandage was wrapped about his head. As Zach neared him, he winced at the sight of the old man's face. The right side was a monstrously swollen, purplish mass. Where the right eye should have been there was only a horizontal slit just beneath a grotesquely canted eyebrow.

"Jesus," Pierre said softly.

Zach reached out and only then did the old man allow himself the luxury of collapsing. As he fell forward, both LeBeau and Zach caught him.

"I've got him," LeBeau insisted. The burly, broad-shouldered foreman ducked his head and slung the old man over his shoulder. He adjusted the old man's weight gently, then frowned with concern at Zach. "Fellow don't weigh more'n a sparrow."

Despite the weight he was carrying, Pierre arrived back at the ranchhouse well before Zach, who ducked inside wearily, his head beginning to spin dangerously, tiny pin-pricks of light dancing before his eyes.

"I'm in here!" called LeBeau from Zach's own bedroom.

Pierre had let the wrangler down onto Zach's bed. The man's eye was closed, and he was breathing very softly, almost imperceptibly. He was not sleeping, however, just resting. Zach pulled a chair over to the side of the bed and sat down.

"Go get Cookie," said Zach. "I think he should look at that bandage."

LeBeau nodded and left the room. Looking down at the wrangler, Zach saw that the old fellow had turned his head slightly and was looking at him.

"You favor your mother," he told Zach softly. "You surely do, and that's a fact. Seen it the first time I laid eyes on you."

"You knew my mother?"

The man's battered face tried to register a smile. At last he managed a slight nod. "Yes, Zach. I knew her."

"What's your name?"

"Silas." The man's voice was soft, so soft Zach had to lean close to hear. "I was working for Dudley when your mother was there." Silas turned his head and looked away. "I drank too much then, too. Otherwise I would have stood up to your father. Always—been sorry I didn't."

"You stood up to him the other day, Silas. You saved my life—and it looks like you paid a fearful price."

Silas looked back at Zach. This time, despite the obvious pain, his face creased into a careful smile. In a voice Zach could barely hear, he said, "Waited a long time for that chance. Glad I didn't miss it."

Then his face went slack and the undamaged eye closed. Cookie entered the room then, his medicine bag—a battered picnic basket—clutched in his hand. Zach got up from the chair.

"See what you can do for him," Zach told the cook. "He's been through a lot."

Nodding grimly, Cookie put his gear down on the seat of the chair and began to unwind the bandage tied around the old man's head. As Zach started to leave the room, Silas opened his eye and called out softly.

Zach returned to the side of the bed. "You better take it easy now, Silas. Let Cookie check your head, then get some sleep. We'll talk later."

"We better talk now."

Zach leaned closer. "Why?"

"Dudley's getting his boys ready to ride on you."

"When?"

"Tomorrow night," the old man said, "when the moon's full. You got to be ready for him."

"You sure?"

"I didn't leave until I was."

"Let Cookie take care of you. We'll talk later."

The old man nodded and closed that one good eye again. His face relaxed. He had come a long way—and on foot—to warn Zach. And now he had.

As Zach hurried out of the room with Pierre, he glanced back at the bed and saw that this time Silas was asleep.

There was silence after Zach finished. As Zach looked around at their faces, he saw that everyone had heard him correctly and understood the plan. What they were trying to do now was decide whether or not to go along.

Dave Snyder spoke first, his voice soft, his whole manner so subdued everyone had to lean forward to hear his words. As he spoke, he kept one hand on the crutch he had used to get into the kitchen and over to the table.

"So you can do as you want, for all I care. I'm selling out to Dudley. My lawyer's dickering with his lawyer in Canyon City right now. I've given notice to my men—to the few who are still left. Dudley Stuart's a madman." He glanced bleakly at Zach. "His son saw to that, pushed him over the edge, he did. I won't stop you men if you go along with this plan of Zach's, but I'm out of it, finished. I'll take what little that man gives me and run."

Using the crutch he pushed himself slowly to his feet, placed his hat on carefully with trembling hands, then leaned toward the door. Zach got to his feet and started to go to the door with him. But Dave waved him back angrily.

"I'll get out without your help, Zach. I don't need your help." He paused for a moment at the door, leaned forward onto his crutch, and looked back at the rest. "Sell out. While you can. You're in the middle of a family feud. No matter what you think about Mary, she was right. She did what she thought was best to save the Diamond Cross."

Then he pulled open the door and plunged out into the night. The table was silent as everyone listened to the sound of Dave's thumping crutch on the porch. Not until they heard his buggy start up, did they lean back and relax.

"I guess maybe it's my turn," said Sue, "since I've been just as outspoken as Mary Snyder was about backing—or not backing—Zach." Her voice was high, nervous. "But I can see now that Dudley Stuart was capable of all this long before Zach arrived in our valley. Perhaps Zach's arrival triggered him a little bit sooner, but, honestly, I feel it was only a matter of time." She looked quickly around her at the intent faces. "You know how he grazed his herds on the Sweetwater Range, no matter how often Dave Snyder protested. And you know how much good Dave's protests did. And the rest of you know what it was like. Whatever Dudley Stuart wanted, he got—him and his crew of gunslicks."

Sullivan nodded gravely. "You are right, Sue. It was only a matter of time before Dudley Stuart came after us."

"Then the Running H is with us?" Zach asked.

"Yes," said Sue. "I'm sure my riders will want to join yours, Zach. They loved my father. More than one of them has come to me and requested that they be allowed to strike back."

"I've only five men left, Zach," said Sullivan. "With my ranch gone and my stock scattered beyond the mountains, I'm finished. But we'll join you in this plan, gladly."

"Eagerly," seconded Tobe Winston, sitting beside Sullivan.

Zach was sitting at the head of the kitchen table with Pierre LeBeau beside him. Cookie was hovering over the coffee pot and the doughnuts waiting on the cast iron stove. Standing behind Cookie were Thompson and Manny Garcia. Zach glanced over at them as Tobe seconded Sullivan's willingness to join the Flying T and saw the grim appreciation light their somber faces. He nodded to them, indicating he was as pleased as they were. The two men left then to tell the rest of Zach's riders.

Zach turned to Sue. "I want you to take Silas into town tomorrow morning and wait there until this is over. Will you do that for me, Sue?"

She hesitated for only a moment, then nodded.

"Good," he said, smiling warmly at her. "That's a load off my mind—and everybody else's, if I'm not mistaken."

"You ain't," growled Sullivan, his dark brows lifting.

"Will you send a rider for my men?" Sue asked. "They'll need to know what's up."

Zach nodded and turned to Pierre. "See to that now, and send a fast rider. We should be ready to move out early tomorrow."

Pierre got up from the table and left the room.

Zach looked back at the others then. "Now to the details," he said, leaning forward and grabbing the sugar bowl and the salt shaker. "Unless I'm mistaken, Dudley will be coming through Black Rock Pass. It's the quickest and most direct route. We'll have men waiting for him there, not many, but enough to let him know we're unhappy at his advance toward the Flying T. But remember, the men are only to harry him and then ride before him, leading him to the ranch."

"Oh, Zach," Sue said softly. "Must you sacrifice all this?"

"It'll keep his men busy. That's what we want. We have a full night's work ahead of us, don't forget."

"I'll take his north herd," said Sullivan.

"Good," said Zach. He looked at Tobe, "And can you round up the south herd, the one he has near the Little Whiskey?"

"No trouble, Zach."

Zach looked grimly at both men. "And you know what to do with all that stock."

Sullivan and Tobe nodded shortly.

"I'm glad you aren't going to do to them what that terrible man did to our stock," said Sue. "That would be too awful."

"We'll just send them over the mountains," agreed Zach. "I know a few ranchers south of the mountains who owe me a favor. I'll give a note to Sullivan and Tobe. The ranchers will know what to do with all that stock. It ain't too far from their own mavericking days."

"What ranches, Zach?" Sullivan asked.

"The T Bar and the Circle. They've got the pens and the pasture to support this many stock for as long as it will take."

"This will wipe out Dudley, Zach," said Tobe.

"Yes, it will," said Zach shortly, "if we have enough men waiting for him when he and his men ride back from the Flying T. I'll want a small party at the pass here," he said, indicating the space behind the bowl and the shaker. "I want them to cut down as many of Dudley's men as they can, then chase them back to the Slash D. That way, there'll be no chance they'll be able to intercept the stock we are removing from their range. They'll be too busy saving their backsides." He looked at Tobe. "That means, Tobe, you'll have to get that south herd north of this point before Dudley's men reach the pass." Zach indicated an area northeast of the salt shaker. "Think you can do it?"

Tobe frowned. "I'd say that's twelve to fifteen miles from the river."

Zach nodded.

"I'll just have to run the fat off them steers is all," Tobe said with a sudden grin.

"Good." Zach leaned back in his chair. "We'll have Dudley wiped out then. And I'll be waiting for him at his ranch."

"Zach!" said Sue, her hand flying to her mouth. "What—what do you mean?"

"Just that, Sue. I'll be waiting for him. Perhaps finally, we can talk sense. We will be two ranchers with no more ranch and no more stock to fall back on. Just two men with an old score to settle. This madness has gone far enough, I'm thinking. I'd like to see it end here."

"A reconciliation, Zach?" Sue asked. "You mean what you said? You want to talk sense with Dudley."

Zach nodded somberly. "If he'll let me."

Suddenly everyone's eyes glanced behind Zach. Zach turned to see Silas moving into the kitchen. He had evidently been in the doorway and had heard what Zach had just proposed. His entire head and one side of his face was swathed in bandages, and he had to reach out to the back of the chair for support as he entered the room.

"Don't do it, Zach!" the old man rasped, his voice low, but harsh enough to carry in the crowded kitchen. "That man'll kill you! You might as well talk sense to a stone wall!"

Zach got to his feet and helped Silas into a chair. He smiled. "Maybe you've got a point, Silas. But I think I'll just have to try it."

"Look at me, Zach," the old man said, reaching up and grabbing Zach by the arm. "Look at me! After you got away, they had to drag him off me. It was like he was attacking your mother all over again—through me!"

Zach shook his head. "I came here to destroy him, Silas. But I have come near destroying everyone in this room. I will stop him! He must be stopped. I know that. But perhaps we can leave the battlefield without both our bodies sprawled across it." Zach looked around the table at Sue, Sullivan, Tobe—and saw the same hope in their eyes.

Sue, especially.

"You're a fool," Silas muttered, shaking his head in despair. "You'll see. You'll see."

Sue left her chair and moved swiftly to the old man's side. She took him gently and helped him back up onto his feet. As she led him from the room, back to his bed, Zach turned and smiled at Cookie. "Let's have some of them fresh doughnuts, Cookie—and some coffee. Some of these men have a hard ride ahead of them tonight."

Dudley turned to look back at the column of riders stretching behind him almost as far as his eyes could see. The long, grassy flat over which they had just ridden was almost blue in the bright wash of moonlight, a sea of grass rippling like water in the gentle night breeze. He turned back around and found the looming sentinels of Black Rock Pass pressing upon him. As they kept riding, the vast shoulders of rock snuffed out the moon.

He glanced at Kid Bunning, who was riding to his left. "Ride ahead. Zach might have riders posted here—if that fool of a traitor ran where you think he did."

The Kid nodded, spurred his horse to a swift lope, and disappeared ahead of them into the darkness of the pass. That Silas might have made it to Zach's ranch to warn him had been carefully considered, and discounted. Silas had been pretty badly beaten up when Dudley had finished with him. He'd crawled off to his rat hole in the horse stable with a bottle Dudley had thrown him. The fact that he was discovered missing only meant to Dudley that he had drunk himself into a self-pitying stupor and crawled off somewhere to die. And good riddance. But the Kid could not be so easily convinced.

Dudley and Nate moved into the pass, great hulking

masses of rock looming on both sides of them. Dudley smiled. Where was the ambush? If Zach knew they were coming, he would have this pass swarming with men.

He glanced back. His line of men were now entering the pass. Dudley glanced at Nate. "The Kid's a mite skittish, after all. Silas has not warned Zach."

The Kid galloped back toward Dudley through the darkness. He swung his horse around and came alongside the rancher. "I didn't see any sign of Zach's men," he said.

"You see? This will be a complete surprise to Zach. He would never think I could do this to him. He'll see."

"Mr. Dudley, we ain't through the pass yet."

"I said he will see, Kid. An army at this pass would not stop me this night!"

As if in answer to his boast, a shot rang out from the rocks far above them. Another shot followed from the other side of the pass. The slugs whined off the rocky ground. Dudley had to steady his horse as the Kid galloped suddenly forward, firing blindly up at the rocky wall.

Pulling up, Dudley turned to his men. They looked like they were ready to turn and high tail it back through the pass. "Come on, you yellow bastards!" Dudley called to them. "We're fish in a barrel here! Ride on through the pass! Follow me!"

Dudley turned and spurred his horse over the rocky ground. He heard the clatter of his men following after him. The dark walls of the pass slid past swiftly, and ahead of him he saw the flat. There had been no more shots, and his spirits rose.

Then, well ahead of him, Dudley saw what he was sure was the Kid chasing two riders. The Kid was occasionally sending a shot after them, but Zach's men were riding with their heads low and their asses high, anxious to put distance between them and Dudley's forces.

Dudley was elated. Zach could not have been warned by Silas! These two men were simply a precautionary pair of lookouts, a natural precaution. There would have been more riders than this if Zach had been warned. Many, many more.

He glanced at Nate, who was keeping pace with him. "You see! Zach won't know what hit him! We'll put a finish to this business tonight!"

Nate nodded grimly, and spurred his horse faster. And then they were through the pass and out onto the flat, their horse's hooves muffled in the deep grass, the two fleeing riders far ahead of the Kid and now barely visible in the moonlight.

Well to the north of Black Rock Pass, Sullivan found Dudley's herd guarded by only two riders. They offered his four riders only token resistance and rode off after a swift, deadly exchange that left one of them leaning forward over his pommel, cradling his left arm as he lit out. The sudden gunfire had lifted the immense herd to its feet as if it were a single animal. Sullivan fired three more shots into the moonlit sky and the herd was off, its pounding hooves filling the night with an ominous thunder.

Tobe had taken six men with him. They splashed across a shallow ford of the Whiskey River and gained the low bluff; drifting closer to the herd, they came upon a campfire burning low. Four Slash D men were curled up in their bedrolls around it. One of them stirred as Tobe pulled up with his six-gun out, and blinked up at him through the darkness. Tobe said softly, "Don't do nothin' foolish and wake your buddies. You're surrounded."

In less than five minutes, the four men were disarmed and sent across the river on foot. Tobe hurried them on their way through the moonlight with a few rounds over their heads, then pointed his six-gun skyward and pumped two quick shots into the night.

The herd was up and off in an instant.

As the herd bolted, Tobe glanced over the sea of plunging backs at the moon. It was still rising. Good! They would make the twelve miles in plenty of time, he was sure—and from that point on, the mountains would be a cinch.

Zach pushed open the bunckhouse door and stole into the low, stifling interior. Enough moonlight was streaming through the grimed windows for him to see that all the bunks were empty. There was a room beyond, however, and he moved swiftly down the row of bunks and tapped the door open with the barrel of his sixgun. The door squeaked on its hinges as it swung.

The room was empty.

Leaving the bunkhouse a moment later, he saw LeBeau darting around the corner of the building, obviously looking for him.

"There's no one in the bunkhouse," Zach said. "What'd you find?"

"Two men. One's guarding the stable, the other's asleep on a cot in the kitchen, a shotgun on the floor beside him. They're both pretty old; don't look any too sharp to me."

"So Dudley left them behind to guard the place—just in case. He certainly is sure of himself. Is his woman in the ranchhouse?"

"Yes, asleep in her own room."

Zach nodded. He knew of her. Her name was Felicia and served as Dudley's housekeeper and wife without benefit of clergy. He did not want her to get hurt.

"Can you take the fellow in the barn?"

LeBeau nodded.

"All right then. Go easy. We may need him. I'll see what I can do about the one in the kitchen."

LeBeau disappeared back into the shadows. Zach gave LeBeau enough time to cross the compound and get to the rear of the stable. Then he slipped through the shadows to the ranchhouse, found one of the kitchen windows, and peered through. Lost in the shadows along the far wall, he could make out the sleeping form of the guard Dudley had left behind to look after the ranchhouse and the woman. Peering closely, he was able to catch the dull glint of the shotgun's barrels where it lay on the floor by the cot.

He mounted the side porch and tried the kitchen door. It swung open to his touch. LeBeau had left it ajar. Stepping into the kitchen, Zach lifted his six-gun from his holster and trained it on the snoring man. Then he kicked the shotgun out from under the cot. When it slammed into the wall, the fellow stopped snoring abruptly and sat up, eyes wide.

Zach cocked his revolver and let the man stare down the weapon's bore. His wrinkled face grew paler than the moonlight that streamed over it.

"Now, now, listen!" the man protested.

"Just stay quiet," Zach warned softly. "I don't want to pull this trigger. I just want you to take the woman out of here."

"Felicia?"

"That's right. Take a carriage and drive her into Canyon City. You think you could do that?"

The old fellow's eyes were as wide as saucers. He nodded eagerly. He would have promised the devil his soul twice over, if Zach was Mephistopheles and that was what he had requested.

"Sit up," Zach said.

Zach checked his person for any hidden armament. Then he asked the fellow for his name. It was Andy.

"Andy, go tell Felicia she's got a visitor and to dress and come out here quietly. Tell her it's Dudley's boy come to see that she gets safely to Canyon City before all hell breaks loose."

As Andy hurried from the kitchen, Zach went to the door and called softly across the compound. At once LeBeau answered.

"I got him, Zach. He's willing to cooperate."

"Tell him to hitch up a buggy. Tell him he hasn't got much time."

Zach went back inside the kitchen and lit a kerosene lamp. He was adjusting its flame when Andy returned with Felicia. She was an old but still handsome woman. A scarf was wound around her head and she was wearing a long, dark green dress that had darker green trim along the bottom of the skirt and lace at her throat. The sleeves were full. It was a fine, handsome dress. Her dark eyes gleamed as she stood in the kitchen regarding him.

"That's pretty fancy finery for the trip into Canyon City," Zach said. "You had better let Andy pack whatever you favor in a traveling bag, if you have one."

"It is already packed," she told Zach, her voice soft. There was not a trace of anger or scorn in it.

"Andy, get it," Zach said.

"It is in the closet," Felicia told the old man, and he disappeared after it. Then she turned back to face Zach. "I have been expecting this moment ever since you returned to this valley, young man. This dress is the only piece of finery your old man ever contrived to buy for me—during the one trip he allowed me to accompany him on to St. Louis."

"Won't you be sorry to leave the Slash D?"

"It has been my prison these many years—and your father my jailer." She smiled at the surprise on Zach's face. "Oh, it was not Dudley's doing entirely. I had no place else to go. I still have no place to go, but it's my last chance to leave him and I must take it. Thank you for that, Zach Stuart."

"I'm releasing you from bondage to him. That it, Felicia?"

"Yes. You are releasing me. But you, it seems, remain in bondage to him—and it is a cruel and destructive bond, reaching out of the past. I think it will destroy you both. You should leave this valley now—as I am doing. Put Dudley Stuart behind you. Forever."

Felicia's words struck Zach as apt, and not a little unsettling. If this woman had been Dudley's companion all these years, he had been a lucky man. Not that Dudley Stuart was a man capable of appreciating someone as wise as this woman appeared to be.

"I can't do that, Felicia," Zach said. "I must finish what Dudley started so many years ago."

She nodded sadly. "I know. That is always so important to you men."

As Andy appeared in the kitchen door with Felicia's packed valise, Zach heard a buggy pulling up in front of the porch. He opened the door and stepped out. LeBeau and a thin, scarecrow of a man were sitting on the front seat. LeBeau handed the man the reins and stepped down.

Felicia followed Zach out and LeBeau helped her into the buggy as Andy hefted the valise into the carriage. Then he climbed into the rear seat behind the woman.

"You two be careful now," Zach warned them. "Take this woman safely in to Canyon City. If you don't, you'll have either Dudley or myself to answer to, here or in Hades."

The man with the reins snapped them hastily. The two horses started off at a brisk gallop. Felicia instinctively brought her hand up to hold her kerchief in place, then looked back at the two men standing in front of the porch steps. She didn't wave or smile and soon her face was lost in the darkness. A moment later the sound of the horses was swallowed up in the night.

"I found some kerosene in back of the blacksmith shop," LeBeau told Zach.

Zach nodded. "Let's get busy, then. We don't want a thing left standing—except that unfinished mansion in among the cottonwoods."

"Why?"

Zach peered across the moonlit yard. He could just barely make out the sun-cured skeleton of the old house partially hidden by the cottonwoods. Looking at it caused an uneasy shudder to pass up his spine. He had felt the same way when first he had ridden into this compound and caught sight of it. "I don't know," he said with a shrug. "I just don't think we should burn it, that's all."

"Okay by me," said LeBeau. "Let me show you where the kerosene is."

Zach nodded and followed LeBeau as he hurried toward the blacksmith Shop. He glanced up at the moon. It was no longer climbing, which meant they would have enough time—if they hurried.

Sixteen

MANNY GARCIA WAS AMONG the last to get out. He wanted to make sure the rest of his men were free of the blazing compound before he made his break for it. So far, everything had gone according to the way Zach had described it.

With Thompson and Silvano leading them, Dudley and his two gunslingers rode hell-bent-for-leather into the compound, guns blazing. As Zach had counseled, Manny and Pilgrim kept up a steady fire from the cookshack, with Sweet, Tex, and Slim keeping things warm from the ranchhouse. Thompson and Silvano had ridden on through, then doubled back and kept up a damaging fire from back of the barns and stables. The idea was to hide the fact that Zach and most of his men were elsewhere, and to that end everyone moved around a lot, firing from as many different vantage points as he could manage. It was not a difficult thing to do as the compound filled up with Slash D riders, each of them hurling lanterns into buildings and onto roofs and firing wildly at anything that moved. The confusion was a great aid to Manny and the others. Once the buildings began to burn, the Slash D men were in plain sight and there were so many of them that it was like shooting fish in a barrel, as Manny shouted to Tex after he saw a Slash D rider peel off his horse. He was sure it was his round that had brought him down.

When Dudley rode over to the burning stables and

began to call his men around him, Manny knew it was time to leave. He gave the word to the others, and soon the men were drifting back into the darkness. They had stashed their horses in a grove a half mile away, and as soon as they were out of the leaping circle of light from the burning buildings, they turned and raced to their waiting mounts.

Manny slipped into a shadow provided by the last wall still standing, the side of the ranchhouse that contained the fireplace. Then, no longer firing, he slipped further away from the flaming compound; He ducked behind a clump of juniper, then raced across the flat until he had outdistanced the unnatural light. As he ran, he glanced up at the sky. The moon was still up, but it was getting lower and would soon sink below the mountains.

Tex had saddled Manny's horse and was waiting in the grove. Manny thanked Tex and mounted up. As he held the reins, he listened for the sound of hooves. Nothing. He rode out of the grove and looked back at the ranch. It was a blazing inferno—made more brilliant by the night that tried to enclose it.

"Dudley knows something's up," Manny told Tex, as he spurred his horse toward the pass. "He got wise when he noticed there were no horses in the stables. I saw him talking about it to his men. He's gonna send them looking for bodies, I'm thinking. When he don't find none, he's goin' to come boilin' out of that compound like a cloud of hornets was on his tail!"

Tex didn't reply. He just nodded and spurred his mount.

Manny looked back over his shoulder. Sure enough! He saw a dark line of riders streaking from the burning compound. "Here they come, Tex!" Manny cried.

Tex glanced back and then began to use his quirt. Manny took just one more look himself, then concentrated on his riding. He was certain they would reach the pass before Dudley's men. And this time, when the Slash D riders tried to blow through the pass, he and Zach's men would whittle them down good and proper.

It was a prospect that pleased Manny.

Riding out of what was left Zach's compound, Dudley was furious. The worst part of it was that the Kid had been right. Silas must have made it to Zach's ranch in time to warn Zach.

Dudley and his men had ridden into a deserted compound, one that had been deliberately opened up to his men. The fire power they had encountered had been just enough to keep them busy and punish them—while it satisfied them that Zach and his men had been caught unawares. Dudley shook his head.

What the hell was that son of his up to, anyway? And then Dudley thought of his own place, and groaned. Not only the ranch, but the stock as well. Zach would not ignore those two herds, not after sacrificing his ranch to the flames like that. At once Dudley decided that as soon as he got beyond the pass, he would split his men and send them after his two herds—if it wasn't already too late.

He thought of Felicia. He had left just two men to guard her and the ranch. Would Zach burn his ranchhouse down with Felicia inside? The thought paralyzed him, and with a shock Dudley Stuart realized what Felicia had come to mean to him. With that realization came the sickening knowledge of his own vulnerability.

He roweled his horse furiously on through the night toward the looming flanks of Black Rock Pass.

Manny found a spot behind a boulder that gave him a perfect view of the trail leading into the pass. He was still perspiring from his climb. Placing his six-gun beside him on a rock shelf, he levered a fresh cartridge into his Winchester, then peered down through the darkness for the first sign of Dudley's men. A splash of moonlight slanted across the trail just before the pass. It would have to suffice. Once into the inky blackness of the pass, Dudley's men would fish in a very dark barrel.

Manny saw and heard nothing for a surprisingly long stretch. He looked around, but could see no one. It didn't mean a thing, he knew. Tex was above him—and every niche and cleft that gave a decent view of the trail was occupied by one of Zach's men, primed and waiting.

The sound of hooves came suddenly on the night wind. With it came the squeak of slapping saddle leather and the jingle of bits. The thunder of the pounding hooves grew. Manny lifted his rifle to his shoulder and sighted on the trail. He saw Dudley streaking into the moonlight, his two gunslicks just behind him on each flank. Remembering Zach's warning not to kill his father, Manny held his fire until Dudley was past, then opened up on the Kid.

He missed. Swearing bitterly, he levered a fresh round into the firing chamber. His shot had been the signal for the others. The rocky walls of the pass opened up like a Chinese New Year. Manny tracked a rider, squeezed the trigger, and saw the man buck as the round burrowed into him. The man rode on into the pass, but Manny knew he would not remain on his horse for long.

He kept up a steady fire. Then all at once the riders were in the pass, swallowed up in the covering darkness. Manny continued to pour fire down until the sound of clattering hooves was gone. It had not taken very long. All that was left were the cries of wounded horses and the groans of perhaps half a dozen men.

Manny got to his feet. He was drained. The excitement had built all during this night to that single moment when Dudley's horsemen had charged into that slant of moonlight and swept on into the pass. Now it was over, and all he felt was an overwhelming weariness. There were men down there on the trail, some dead, the lucky ones wounded, and fine horses that would have to be shot.

He shook his head, slipped his revolver into his holster,

and carrying his Winchester, started down the dark trail. Manny knew something about this business Zach had with his father. He understood why Zach had to return to this valley to settle accounts. But for the first time, as he got closer to those wounded men below him, he asked himself if maybe all this bloodletting was not too high a price to pay for settling accounts.

Perhaps, like him, a man was lucky when he *didn't* know who his father was.

Mark Thompson was mounted and waiting with Silvano, Gordo, and Tully on the other side of Black Rock Pass. They waited in the shadows of a cottonwood grove as Dudley's men poured out onto the flat. In the light of the waning moon, it was difficult to see how many had made it through Manny's ambush; but it looked to Thompson as if Dudley's forces had been cut almost in half. Nudging his horse to the edge of the grove, Thompson could make out three riders just barely able to keep themselves in the saddle, and two men riding double.

Once Dudley was beyond the pass and well into the flat, he pulled up. He sent two groups of riders off; one went north, the other south. Thompson grinned. Old Dudley was wise by this time and was sending his men after his herds. But it was too late, Thompson knew. What was that about locking the barn door after the horses had been stolen?

Thompson waited until the two groups of riders had been swallowed up in the darkness, then turned to his waiting men and nodded. With six-guns out, they bolted from the cottonwoods and galloped across the moonlit flat toward Dudley and his few remaining riders. Waiting until they were almost within range, they opened up on Dudley and the remnants of his weary army.

Tully let out a blood-curdling yell he had borrowed from an Apache. It was almost comical, the way Dudley and his riders started whaling at their mounts. This had been one hell of a night for old Dudley, Thompson thought to himself as he fired another salvo after the fleeing riders.

He was enjoying himself immensely.

As he rode beside his enraged boss, Kid Bunning found a difficult to hide his jubilation. Nate Claw was back there in that pass. The Kid had seen Nate get hit. And it was a bad one. One minute the son of a bitch was riding along beside him, his six-gun out as he fired blindly, futilely up at Zach's men. The next moment half his head was gone and he was peeling backward off his horse.

Just like that—and now the Kid was second in command to Dudley! When Dudley let the Kid take care of Zach—and there was little doubt that after this night Dudley would unleash him—the old bastard would have no one else to stand by him as he rebuilt his power in this valley. The Kid would be his heir some day. After all, who else did Dudley have to leave his spread to? Not that woman Felicia, certainly.

The thought warmed the Kid. He suddenly felt good about the old son of a bitch. He wanted to protect him. He really did. Alive, Dudley was his route to becoming something substantial. He would no longer just be someone's hired gun. The Kid's thoughts raced ahead, filling him with visions of himself astride the best horseflesh money could buy, a respectable woman in his kitchen and in his bed, greeting the townsmen whenever he rode into Canyon City. He would no longer have to swim in this sea of hatred that walled him off from every other human being. Perhaps he could let his guard down once in a while, even let someone laugh at him or slap him on the back too hard. And then just let it pass.

That would be nice. It was difficult, so damn difficult, always having to be tougher than the next guy.

"Damn it!" cried Dudley. "Them bastards are gaining on us!"

The Kid glanced back as he rode. He had good eyes,

even at night. Some told him they thought he had cat's eyes. Maybe he did. What he saw now encouraged him. There were only four men on their tail.

"Sam! Pete! Jake!" the Kid cried out. "Peel off! They ain't but four of them!"

The Kid knew his men. Without a word of protest, they cut their horses away from the main body of riders. Tracing a tight circle, they came together again with the Kid in the lead—heading right for the four riders. Six-guns out, they began throwing lead at the oncoming men and saw them turn, heading north.

"Get the bastards!" cried the Kid exultantly. He knew Dudley could not help but notice how neatly he had turned the tables on Zach's men. The pursuers were now the pursued.

Old Dudley sure as hell would want to show his appreciation for that.

Seventeen

ZACH HAD PROCEEDED WITH great deliberation. First he and Pierre had released all the horses from the stables, and even sent the chickens clucking into the night. After that they had methodically poured kerosene around the foundations and over the rooms of the bunkhouse, the cookshack, the ranchhouse, finishing up finally with the three privies. Then they had set off each building carefully, making sure that no walls would be left standing. Even the corrals' fencing was set ablaze.

Now they stood among the cottonwoods, the unfinished mansion looming behind them in the darkness, watching the flames leaping skyward. The heat was intense. The leaves on the cottonwoods were browning and twisting in the blast. Shading his eyes with his right arm, Zach watched the tallest barn collapse in an explosion of flaming embers that arced high into the night. Where they came down, small fires raced through the dry grass until extinguished by cart tracks or patches of stony soil.

It was a hellish sight. Zach glanced at Pierre. The man was staring at the roaring destruction as somberly as Zach. The smaller stable next to the barn collapsed with a roar, sending still more flaming embers rocketing skyward. For the moment the heat grew even more intense.

Above the sharp cracking of beams and the shuddering

roar of the flames, Zach heard the unmistakable sound of pounding hoofs.

"Keep out of sight back here," Zach told Pierre. "Let me play this my way. When I've finished, whichever way it goes—do what suits you."

Pierre nodded, then hunkered down with his back to a tree, his rifle cradled in his arms. Zach walked to the edge of the grove in time to see Dudley break through the ring of fire, a small crowd of riders on his heals. Many of Dudley's men were wounded and were able to pull up their mounts only with great difficulty. As Zach watched, one of the riders slipped slowly, helplessly off his horse. Two others were riding double. One of them slipped down and went to the aid of the man who had fallen.

Dudley, his shoulders back, his high brow gleaming in the blazing light, was looking slowly around him at the blazing compound. He rode closer to the ranchhouse. It was the last building Zach had set ablaze and was still intact, with the flames only now breaking through the roof.

"Felicia!" the old man cried anxiously.

Zach levered a fresh cartridge into the firing chamber of his Winchester and stepped out of the cottonwoods. "She's not there, Dudley!"

Dudley swung around, his face tight with rage. He spurred his mount toward Zach; those of his men who were still able nudged their mounts after him. Zach stood his ground calmly as Dudley pulled up a few yards from him, his men circling around him, their eyes glittering in the blazing light.

Dudley loomed threateningly over Zach. "You say she's not there?" he asked, glaring somberly down at his son. "Where is she?"

"Those two men you left to guard her have taken her to Canyon City," Zach replied. "She had her bags packed. Said it was the first good chance she had to leave here. Seems it was what she wanted."

Dudley took the news grimly, blinking only once—as if

he were downing a shot of ten-minute whiskey. "Damn you, Zach. You ain't destroyed me yet, but you're making a fine effort. It's just between you and me now, ain't it."

Zach nodded.

Dudley's eyes narrowed. "I see you left that whip behind this night."

In the light from the burning buildings, Zach could see clearly the livid stripes that furrowed Dudley's face. Many of those scars would remain, visible reminders of Zach's punishment. In his dreams, all during those long years of waiting to return to this valley—and to his father—Zach had imagined himself branding his father in just this way. He had wanted all who looked upon Dudley's countenance to see mirrored in it the scarred, livid ugliness of the old rancher's soul. Now Zach saw that he had succeeded in this beyond his wildest imaginings. He should have been exultant, satisfied at last.

Instead, he felt only weariness.

"That's right, Dudley. I left the whip behind."

"You willing to leave it at that, then?" The old man asked, slumping in his saddle. "If my ruination was what you wanted, you have it. After this night's business, there's no way I can keep the lid on. I have already been warned by my friends in the capital. We'll soon have a deputy U.S. marshal nosing around this valley. There'll be no place in it then for the Slash D brand."

"Yes, that's what I wanted. But it is not all I want."

"Damn you, mister. What more do you want? My life? I warn you. I'll sell that dearly and take you with me if I must—and we'll finish this business in Hell!"

Glancing around him at the flames still leaping into the night, at the hot blasts carried past them on the night air, at the perspiring faces of Dudley and his riders—Zach smiled sardonically up at his father. "And what makes you think you're not there already, Dudley?"

"What do you *want?*"

"Kid Bunning."

"No. He's my right hand."

"Then I want that right hand."

"What will you do with him?"

"He shot down my best friend, Dudley. He led those riders that burned out the Belle Fourche. A lot of townsmen can still hear Jane and her girls inside screaming. A whiskey-soaked cowpoke was abroad that night. He saw the Kid leading those riders into Canyon City. I want the Kid to stand trial."

'The Kid was sent on my orders."

"I'm sure that will come out in the trial."

"And if I don't let you have him?"

"I'll take you—right now, Dudley. You said you'd sell your life dearly. Well, let's see *how* dearly."

"My men will cut you down."

"Do you think I care?" Zach shifted the rifle in his hand deftly so that the barrel was pointing at Dudley's heart, while Zach's finger rested on the trigger.

"So, what if you do succeed finally in killing me, Zach? Do you think that will end it? Do you think what I did to your mother ended it for me?" He smiled bitterly. "It don't kill you, you know. Won't even weaken you much. So you just go on living. *That's* the hell of it."

"I want the Kid—or you."

"If you kill me, Zach, you'll do me a favor. But I don't want what that will do to you."

"What makes you think I'd care that much, Dudley?"

Dudley straightened in his saddle and looked down unhappily at Zach. "Because there's more than just me inside you. There's your mother in there, too."

At that moment the Kid rode into the blazing compound with three other riders. He rode directly over to Dudley. He smiled when he saw Zach surrounded. Pulling up beside his boss, he said, "Well, look what we got here."

"Drop your gunbelt, Kid," Zach told him. "You're coming with me."

"Like hell I am. I'm stayin' right here, alongside your old man. You ain't licked us yet, mister—and right now we got you by the short hair." He turned to Dudley. "You caught the son of a bitch in the act, huh?"

Dudley shook his head. "He was waiting here. For me. And for you."

The Kid leaned over his pommel to peer closer at Zach. As he did so, he drew his Smith & Wesson. "Well, here we are, Zach. Now, you just throw down that rifle and maybe I won't kill you on the spot."

Dudley pulled his horse back so that he was facing the Kid directly. "Put away that gun, Kid. Do as Zach says. You're going with him."

The Kid was stunned, his face suddenly livid. "What the hell do you mean?"

"Zach thinks you should stand trial. But don't worry. I'll see to it."

"Stand trial! For what?"

"The burning of the Belle Fourche—and for killing Handler."

"And you'll fix *that?* There ain't a soul in that town wouldn't pay to see me hang!"

"You heard me. Drop your gunbelt. You're going with Zach."

"Like hell, I am!"

Dudley looked around at his men. "Disarm him!" he ordered. "Now!"

"You double-crossin' son of a bitch!" the Kid cried furiously.

As he shouted he swiftly hauled his gleaming six-gun around and sent two rounds into Dudley's chest. Two neat holes were suddenly stamped in his white shirt front. In the bright glare from the still burning buildings, Zach saw the old rancher's body buck sharply, twice. Yet, somehow, he remained upright. A look of grim astonishment swept over his face. Then—his powerful, gnarled hands still clinging to his reins—he began to slip crookedly from his saddle.

All this Zach noted in an instant—as he plunged past his father's horse and reached up to haul the Kid out of his saddle. With a pleased grunt, the Kid clubbed Zach on his recently wounded shoulder with the barrel of his six-gun. Zach felt the sudden, disabling pain radiating out from his shoulder and slipped backward to the ground, his head spinning.

Dimly, he was aware of the struggle around him as the others tried to corral the Kid. Looking up through pain-slitted eyes, Zach saw the Kid beating his way through the encircling riders, and then spurring his mount toward the cottonwoods. Dudley's men were too astonished by this sudden turnabout—and too wary of the Kid's brutality—to make any real effort to overtake him.

Zach staggered to his feet. His shoulder felt like someone had rammed a branding iron through it.

Ignoring the discomfort, Zach snatched up his rifle. Dudley was on the ground, a concerned, puzzled circle of his men staring down at him. Frowning at the unexpected turmoil this sight aroused in him, Zach turned and raced toward the cottonwoods. The dancing light from the flames behind him turned the stand of cottonwoods into a nightmarish confusion of shifting light and shadow.

A shot came from his left. He heart a thrashing sound, which slowly faded. Following the sound he soon came to the Kid's abandoned horse. A moment later, he came across Pierre. The man had propped himself up against a tree. He was alert and pleased to see Zach.

"I pulled him off his horse," Pierre said. "I should have had him, but he was too quick for me. He got me in the side."

"Which way did he go?"

"Toward that unfinished building back there."

Zach nodded, hesitating at the sight of Pierre's blood-soaked shirt.

"You go ahead, Zach. I'll be all right. The bullet passed right on through. I ain't bleedin' like I should." LeBeau smiled wanly.

Zach patted him on the shoulder and slipped deeper

into the grove, heading for the shadowy bulk of the unfinished mansion. The ranch buildings had about burned themselves out by this time and the darkness was almost complete. When he got close to the pale, skeletal remains of the mansion, he found it had a kind of sad magnificance—like the persistence of hope when all hope is gone.

He was crossing a short, weed-choked lawn when a shot rang out from a second story window. The round richocheted off a tree just behind him. Zach darted swiftly up onto the spacious veranda and plunged into the pitch-black interior. He flattened himself against an inner wall and listened. After a long moment, heavy footsteps moved cautiously across the floor just above his head, then paused. Following the sound with his eyes, Zach was able to make out the rough, unfinished beginnings of a staircase that led up to a square opening in the ceiling.

Slowly, carefully, he lowered himself to the floor, stretched himself full length, steadied his gun hand with his left and trained his gunsight on the dark opening. And waited. The darkness in the place was no longer so complete as his eyes grew accustomed to it. Shadowy doorways materialized on all sides of him, and he saw the beginnings of a long hall with a boarded window at the far end of it.

A movement in the darkness at the head of the staircase caught his attention. Holding his breath, aware that the blow on his left shoulder had truly damaged him, possibly reopening his wound, he prayed silently that the Kid would move down the stairway just a few more steps. There was another movement, and this time a shadowy form took shape against the stairs. Zach saw two legs. Possibly the Kid saw Zach's sprawled figure and concluded he had struck him earlier with that shot from the window.

But no. He could not think that. He must have heard the bullet ricochet off the tree.

The Kid moved further down the stairs. Zach's

gunsight rested on his chest. Zach debated the virtues of waiting for a head shot. He should not have. Moving with sudden, deadly swiftness, the shadowy form shifted. Zach caught the dull glint of the Kid's Smith & Wesson. A fierce detonation thundered in the dark hallway. The slug creased Zach's forehead, the impact rendering him nearly senseless. Only dimly was Zach aware of his own weapon thundering in his hand. The gun jumped like something alive, his thumb cocking the weapon with a mindless automatism. Then the Kid's body plunged down out of the blackness upon him.

The Kid was flailing at him brutally, gasping and cursing violently, his fury arousing Zach as nothing else could. Punching back, Zach rose slowly to his feet, the Kid staying with him, trading punch for punch. For a solid minute the two stood in the darkness of the hallway at the foot of the stairway trading punches like two blind goliaths—until gradually Zach became aware that he was striking out at a dimming, collapsing figure; that the floor beneath his feet was slippery with blood—as were his own two fists.

The Kid abruptly collapsed forward onto Zach, his head resting heavily on Zach's sore left shoulder. He continued to paw automatically at Zach, but his punches had lost all sting. The man was winding down like some terrible toy designed only to kill.

Zach pushed him upright, then flung him back as he became aware of the warm sweet slick of blood pulsing from a gaping wound in the Kid's chest. The Kid cried out as he went slamming backward into a door, then collapsed face down inside a room leading off the hallway. Zach watched the still-moving figure, his hand reaching out to the doorjamb for support. The Kid grew still at last.

Zach became aware of a thudding pulse in his temples. His breath was coming in short, sharp, painful gasps. And he was soaking wet, as much from blood as from perspiration. He clung to the doorway with both hands as the dark, hellish interior of the place spun sickeningly around him.

At last his throbbing temples grew quiet and he was breathing easier. The pain in his shoulder slackened. He stepped into the room, past the still body, and reached out for a lamp he could see on a small table. It took him a while to fish a sulfur match out of his pocket and light the lamp.

He found himself astonished at what the sudden light revealed. The room was furnished with a comfortable upholstered leather chair. It faced a fireplace which had obviously been used recently. A thick carpet lay on the floor and there was a large four-poster bed in the far corner, with an oak dress alongside. On the dresser, neatly and immaculately displayed, was a comb and brush set. And on either side of this were photographs of Zach's mother—and with her a younger, more handsome Dudley Stuart.

The photographs—one of them was a daguerreotype—were faded and sere; but the happiness and hope Zach saw reflected in the faces of both his father and his mother filled him with a sudden, choking sadness. He looked blindly about the room and saw other pictures of his mother, some on the mantel over the fireplace, others on the wall facing the upholstered chair.

There was no doubt in Zach's mind whose heavy frame over the years had molded the shape of this single leather chair and whose eyes had looked upon those faded images of his mother—alone here in this room, hidden away in the stillborn ruins of a mansion that would never echo to the footsteps and laughter of the woman he loved.

Swiftly, Zach bent, grabbed the Kid's legs, and dragged him from the room. Pulling the door shut, he left the mansion and hurried back through the cottonwoods.

He was thinking of his father—of the way he had looked as those two bullets had planted themselves in his chest.

Eighteen

THE BLACKENED RUINS WERE still glowing, the smoke still twisting into the brightening sky. Zach had sent the slightly wounded LeBeau out to call in his men, and now his riders were trailing in, nervously eyeing the Slash D riders milling aimlessly about in the still smoldering wreckage. The riders said little to one another, perhaps ashamed at the violence and destruction their arms had fashioned this night.

Still on the ground where he had fellen, Dudley Stuart was dying. Zach knelt beside him, while three of Dudley's riders sat their horses a little distance away out of respect for the privacy of Dudley Stuart and his son.

Dudley Stuart began to cough. The effort caused him to groan painfully and open his eyes. He saw Zach leaning over him and managed a weak smile.

"The Kid," he said softly. "You got him?"

Zach nodded.

"I would not have let him kill you."

"You shouldn't have turned him over to me like that. And maybe I shouldn't have made you."

Dudley nodded slightly. "No, you shouldn't have. But—we do terrible things, don't we, Zach. Terrible things. And then we're sorry—only it's too late. Always too late." The old rancher turned his head so that he could see through the cottonwoods at the unfinished mansion. "You didn't burn it, did you."

"No," Zach said.

"There's a room in there, Zach. It would have been your mother's bedroom." He looked back at Zach. "Burn it. Burn it all, Zach. Wipe the slate clean."

Zach nodded.

Dudley reached up and grabbed Zach's arm with a strength that was surprising. "I loved her, Zach," he said fiercely. "I loved your mother. I just wasn't very smart about it. It was too much for me. I didn't know how to handle it—to believe it. But since that night, not a day has passed when I didn't think of her and realize just how much I loved her. And of what I done."

Zach didn't know what to say.

Dudley released Zach's arm and closed his eyes. The effort of those passionate words had drained him. Now a thin ribbon of blood seeped from one corner of his mouth. Zach leaned closer. The man's eyes opened slowly. He smiled.

"I'm glad—you came back," he whispered softly. Now Zach had to lean closer to hear him. "I never knew about you. I never knew—all them years—that she lived. It was cruel, Zach. Awful cruel. But now you ended it for me. For that, I thank you—"

His eyes closed again. This time the heavy lids seemed to sink deep into their sockets. The man's face grew slack. Zach placed his hand on the old rancher's chest. It was as still as the earth on which he lay.

Zach got up and removed his hat. The riders behind Zach dismounted and walked closer, taking off their hats also and looking down in some awe at the still figure. Soon, most of the other riders had gathered around.

At last Zach spoke to LeBeau and Manny Garcia, and they set to work fashioning a shroud out of the dead man's slicker. They slung his body over his horse and tied him on for the ride in to Canyon City. Then Zach found a still burning beam among the charred and smoldering remains of a stable and carried it through the cottonwoods, into the mansion. He did not bother to remove the

Kid's body as he fired the tinder-dry building. For a while he stood in among the trees and watched the leaping flames as they robbed the bright morning sky of its glow.

Zach turned about and found his way once more back through the cottonwoods.

The train's whistle alerted Zach. He glanced down the track and saw the engine's white plume of smoke puffing into the sky. Looking back at Sue and Silas, he smiled.

"Thanks for seeing me off," he said.

"Sure wish you weren't going," Silas said. "Seems to me you ain't got no reason to go now. Them charges being dropped, and all."

"You just give Sue a hand with all them cowhands she'll be ordering around," Zach said, "and stay out of the bottle."

He winked at Sue.

"Silas is right, you know," the girl said. "There's no reason for you to go now. It's all been cleared up. You don't really have to sell your land to the rest of us. There's plenty of room now in the valley for another rancher."

"Thanks, Sue. But I think this is best."

Zach smiled as he spoke so she would not read the turmoil in his heart. He wanted to stay. And he knew Sue wanted him to stay. He was very close to loving Sue Torgeson. But there were memories alive in this valley that would never leave either of them in peace. All they would remember finally whenever they looked into each other's eyes was the ruin and tragedy Zach had brought upon so many—and upon Sue, expecially—from the moment he stepped down off that train on a rain-swept spring morning.

He had given it a lot of thought these past weeks, waiting for the legalities to be settled, and for his land to be parceled out to the members of the Association that wished to buy it. What he had realized finally was that there was no way he could have done it any differently. He had simply played the hand that had been dealt him. He knew that, and he was confident Sue understood it as well.

The train was thundering past the platform now. Its great wheels thundered on the rails. As the coaches clicked past, Zach picked up his gladstone and turned back to Sue and Silas for the last time.

Both were watching him with somber expressions; and he could see the acceptance of this parting in Sue's eyes. She knew it was best. She understood as well as Zach why he had to board this train and move on. Suddenly Sue stepped forward and flung her arms around Zach's neck and hung on tightly for a long moment. When she stepped back, there were unashamed tears in her eyes. Zach turned to Silas and stuck out his hand. Silas took it silently and shook it.

Zach turned and swung up into the train, waved once, and entered the coach. A moment later, as Canyon City slipped behind him, he caught a glimpse of the bright mountains ahead. It occurred to him then that the bondage Felicia had spoken of was gone now. Zach was no longer a hostage to his past. His return to this valley had freed him from that, at least, and for the first time he had a future that was his entirely, one no longer determined by old hatreds and past wrongs.

Zach Stuart leaned back in his seat, his keen eyes studying with sudden interest the mountain peaks shimmering in the distance.